FIRE ON THE RUNWAY

A PAUL SHENSTONE MYSTERY

Fire on the Runway

MEL BRADSHAW

DUNDURN
TORONTO

Editor: Allister Thompson
Design: Jesse Hooper
Printer: Webcom

Library and Archives Canada Cataloguing in Publication

Bradshaw, Mel, 1947-
    Fire on the runway : a Paul Shenstone mystery / by Mel Bradshaw.

Issued also in electronic formats.
ISBN 978-1-4597-0335-3

    I. Title.

PS8603.R332F57 2013   C813'.6   C2012-904649-3

1 2 3 4 5   17 16 15 14 13

We acknowledge the support of the **Canada Council for the Arts** and the **Ontario Arts Council** for our publishing program. We also acknowledge the financial support of the **Government of Canada** through the **Canada Book Fund** and **Livres Canada Books**, and the **Government of Ontario** through the **Ontario Book Publishing Tax Credit** and the **Ontario Media Development Corporation**.

Care has been taken to trace the ownership of copyright material used in this book. The author and the publisher welcome any information enabling them to rectify any references or credits in subsequent editions.

J. Kirk Howard, President

Printed and bound in Canada.

VISIT US AT
Dundurn.com | Definingcanada.ca | @dundurnpress | Facebook.com/dundurnpress

Dundurn	Gazelle Book Services Limited	Dundurn
3 Church Street, Suite 500	White Cross Mills	2250 Military Road
Toronto, Ontario, Canada	High Town, Lancaster, England	Tonawanda, NY
M5E 1M2	LA1 4XS	U.S.A. 14150

For dearest Carol

We live in a fireproof house,
far from inflammable materials.
A vast ocean separates us from Europe.
— SENATOR RAOUL DANDURAND,
CANADIAN DELEGATE TO THE LEAGUE OF NATIONS

Up Front

THIRTY-THREE KILLS.

Eight years after the Armistice, thousands of vets
— even police officers like myself, who still had charge
of firearms — were able to go weeks or months at a time
without thinking about soldiering. There were so many
newer things to think about — sheiks and flappers,
insulin and contract bridge, the radio-relayed voices
of Al Jolson and Binnie Hale. Not to mention feats of
aviation. Alcock and Brown's crossing of the Atlantic,
Alan Cobham's flight to Australia, and the exploits of
Christopher "Kip" Whitehead.

But for me, with Kip it was different. He hadn't
let his war record define him, but even to say as much
was to bring that record to mind.

Unlike so many ace fighter pilots, Whitehead
hadn't let peace throw him into a tailspin. Not that
I was on intimate terms with the man. I'd only met
him at Remembrance Day observances — plus that

one time when as investigating officer I'd helped him recover a rather costly stolen car. But as far as I could see he'd mastered the art of taking orders from bureaucrats untried in battle. No one who'd partied with him suggested he was either boozy or quarrelsome. Much as he'd taken to combat, Kip appeared not to have brought back to this side of the Atlantic any surplus aggressive spirit that could injure his countrymen, his loved ones, or himself.

Aggressive spirit he'd had in spades in wartime, the measure of it trumpeted in every news story. Thirty-three Austro-Hungarian pilots machine-gunned or driven down out of control. Or burned alive in their machines. Even allowing for some padding of the numbers, that's a toll to make you think. In peacetime, the only man to match it would be the public hangman. I'm not calling Whitehead an executioner. He was a pilot; we were at war. Where he sat, it was kill or be killed. But to wear that number for the rest of your life...? I'm not sure how I'd have borne up.

We in the infantry didn't especially keep track, neither I nor the soldiers I led. Sometimes you just didn't know if the bullet or bomb you sent off found its man. And then the targets were less valuable. In the air, every kill meant the destruction of a plane worth upwards of £5,000. Every enemy pilot was an officer, an asset in whom specialized training had been invested. Can you compare those prizes with the conscript private in his first trench, his few, cheap weapons to be stripped from his corpse for reuse by the next to die?

I'm not saying Kip's conquests were any cause for regret. I admired them. As a fighter on the same side (albeit on a different front), I was grateful for them. At the same time, mention of his name tended to prepare my ear for sounds of battle.

Be they ever so faint.

Chapter 1

I FELT LIKE THE only witness. Lifting my eyes from the *Examiner*, I looked out of the Queen streetcar just in time to see a window blown out of the end of the Beaconsfield Hotel. No one else seemed to notice. The accompanying blast, I'll give you, was muffled — not crisp like an engine backfiring in the street or one of the pyrotechnic bangs in the sky on Victoria Day. Still, it surprised me that no other passengers reacted. Perhaps they were preoccupied with the September heat wave, or the jobs they were rolling towards for the last time before the Labour Day long weekend, or what appliances were on sale at Eaton's department store. My own thoughts were running along less tranquil lines. I'd just been reading an article about one of our war heroes.

Christopher "Kip" Whitehead had just completed the first non-stop solo flight from Calgary to Toronto. Or was it the fastest? Aeronautical records were being set monthly, and it was hard even for newsmen to keep up. Either way, the dashing RCAF wing commander and former fighter ace was adding to the prestige of his country's spanking new air force. Fret as the brass might about the leave he required for his "stunts," the public loved him — loved him all the more for the easy way he bore their attention. Take this day's page-one photo of him standing in front of the confection of wires and wooden struts that made up his Curtiss Canuck biplane. His hair's still tousled from the leather flying helmet he's just peeled off. You can see it dangling from his left hand. His right arm is squeezing the waist of his young wife, and they're grinning at each other like a couple of dizzy kids. At the same time, you can tell she's a postwar, modern woman: her no-nonsense grip on the wrench in her right hand shows that, like her sisters that kept the munitions factories running, she's ready for man's work — specifically for work on her man's machines. Envious? Let's just say my own social calendar for the holiday weekend still had a few blanks.

I was happy for him. Kip Whitehead was on top of the world, even before his next announced venture: a flight to the North Pole. A story of high spirits and adventure — danger, but not combat. And yet I never forgot that Kip's first fame and achievement was as a warrior.

That's where my mind was when at 8:45 on a Friday morning — with no more than a dull thump and a tinkle — glass from one of the hotel's second-storey windows burst out in shards to fall onto the roof of the butcher shop adjoining. Dark smoke puffed from the opening, smudging the cloudless blue sky.

I was on my way to work, late. What awaited me at police headquarters was a desk piled with reports of traffic fatalities. The city had few more roads than when I'd joined the force, but there were six times as many cars negotiating them. To keep things moving, the speed limit had been raised from fifteen to twenty miles an hour, which meant carelessness more often resulted in death. My current assignment was to recommend whether manslaughter charges should be laid against any of the drivers. As such charges rarely resulted in convictions, it seemed like futile bother. Here, in contrast, was a situation requiring immediate action. This was more like the work I'd signed on for. I showed my badge to the conductor, who signalled the motorman to stop the car and let me out.

The unscheduled halt attracted more passenger attention than the explosion itself.

"What's wrong? What's the trouble?" A woman seated by the rear doors tugged at my sleeve while pinning a squirming child to her lap with her other hand.

"Nothing to worry about," I assured her as the doors closed behind me.

Traffic was heavy but slow, and my raised palm — police training, day one — persuaded drivers to let me cross the street.

As far as I was concerned, there was plenty to worry about. First, the possibility of life-threatening injuries, which counselled a speedy inspection of the site. Second, the possibility of further explosions, which counselled caution. I was hoping whatever else was involved that nothing had caught fire; happily, when I got my nose through the door, no whiff of smoke reached it.

The Beaconsfield, located on that stretch of Queen between the Parkdale railway station and the Provincial Lunatic Asylum, looked to be a second-rate hotel on its way to third-rate. I'd lived in worse. The deskman was no more alert than you'd expect. He knew nothing of an explosion. He knew of nothing on the second floor capable of exploding. I got him to call Police Station Number Six for a couple of constables, but didn't wait for them before climbing the stairs. The elevator was signed "Out of Order."

Cursing the regulations that forced me to wear a wool suit in this heat, I went up at a run.

The second floor corridor was empty at the stairwell end. But when I looked left, at the farther, eastern end, I made out a man lying on the floor and another standing over him. I couldn't see a weapon in the standing man's hands. You can bet, though, I watched them closely as I walked towards him. My own service revolver was in my desk at City Hall, more than two miles down the street.

The combination of hard shoe leather and carpetless floor made stealth impossible. The standing man turned at the sound of my footsteps.

"Police," I called. "Step back, please."

The standing man turned a pale, shocked face my way. He looked about ten years my junior, no more than twenty-four or -five. He didn't move.

At the same time, a door to my right opened, hinged ahead of me so I couldn't see in.

"What is it, Floyd?" a high, anxious voice called from the room.

"Stay inside, Jenny. Shut the door, and go back inside, there's my girl."

The door closed partway.

"Do as he says, ma'am." I had come level now with the doorknob. I pulled it till the door clicked shut, then took a step back. "Now, Floyd, walk towards me."

He did so, looking grateful for direction.

"Good. Do you have any weapons, Floyd?"

"Weapons? No. Oh God, he's a mess. I can't tell you. He's just ..."

"Okay," I said. "I'm going to have a look. Go back in your room and stay there with Jenny. Shut the door and wait until someone comes to question you. Will you do that?"

"Are you really police?"

"Detective Sergeant Paul Shenstone."

He went into his room and shut the door.

I watched to see it didn't open again as I approached the man on the floor, although I was pretty sure by now that Floyd and Jenny were innocent honeymooners and that simple curiosity had brought Floyd into the hall when he heard the explosion.

I walked around the man on the floor and crouched down. He was a smallish man, narrow shouldered and not more than five foot five or six inches tall. He looked as if he'd been caught holding a grenade. His right hand and wrist were gone, the arm partially severed at the shoulder. Shrapnel had shattered his lower jaw and left his grey shirt front a bloody mess. Once convinced that the compression of the blast had flattened his lungs for good, I lost interest in his lesser wounds and turned my attention to his surroundings. Only half the glass of the hall window had been blown out, that mainly at chest level and to the side away from Queen Street. The door of the end room on that side of the hall had been knocked off its hinges and lay not quite flat inside the room. At the end farthest from me, something was propping it up. I stood and stepped closer to have a look. What I saw restored my sense of urgency. Bare legs and the lower part of a body skirted in rust-coloured fabric were sticking out from under the door.

I grabbed the bottom of the door and, twisting to the right, leaned it up against the jamb, uncovering the rest of the woman. She lay on her stomach, her left cheek to the floor, her left arm bent above her head as if to fend off the falling door. I didn't see any blood or feel any dampness beyond perspiration when I ran my hands underneath her. But her skin from ankles to eyelids was the colour of mashed potatoes. Her eyes remained closed when I turned her over. She was breathing, at least. Shallowly, but breathing.

I glanced down the empty hall and listened. Traffic noise drifted up from Queen Street; no sound of movement came from the building. More men with explosives might be lurking behind closed doors, but I shoved that risk to the back of my mind as I tried to coax the casualty back to consciousness.

"Open your eyes now." I cradled her face between my hands and turned it towards me. While nothing could feel cool at this day's temperatures, her skin lacked any animal warmth. "Can you hear me? Miss! What are we going to call you?"

No answer. I remembered the number I'd seen on the door.

"Knock, knock, Room 29. Time to wake up in there."

Not even a flicker of the shades.

I let her head settle back onto the floor and picked up her left wrist. Her arm was loose and limp. "Or I could call you Raggedy Ann," I said. "Do you have a pulse?" I groped for what I thought was the radial artery. Nothing. Anxiously, I pressed harder, hard enough to obliterate any pulse there was. I wiped the sweat out of my eyes and tried again. There — a feeble excuse for a pulse. "That's it, miss," I urged. "Keep pumping."

I gave her hand a reassuring squeeze. Reassuring to me at least; she didn't give any sign one way or the other. She was breathing; she had a heartbeat. Still, we didn't want her slipping deeper into coma. I gave the flesh on the inside of her left forearm a pretty hard pinch. Her arm pulled away. I pinched again. This time, besides pulling away, she rubbed the place with her right hand.

A plaintive string of syllables came from her mouth. I couldn't make anything of them. They were either a foreign language or disoriented gibberish. We were getting somewhere, though. I guess I was feeling less apprehensive about her, because I took half a second to notice that it was a sweet mouth, with a slight peak in the middle of the upper lip.

"Do you speak English?" I asked her. "I'm betting your eyes are blue."

Miss 29's eyes opened. They were grey, without a trace of blue, a grey I'd never seen in eyes before; they looked like they came from a hundred million miles away. They weren't focusing yet.

I moved my hand from side to side in front of her face. "Try to follow my finger with your eyes," I said.

She said something I couldn't get. Her eyes didn't move.

"What's all this?" A gruff, none too happy voice behind me.

I turned to see the broad figure of a uniformed policeman looming over me, with the less substantial desk clerk hovering in the background.

I showed the copper my badge, which transformed his demeanour from scowling to deferential. "Looks like a Mills bomb killed one, concussed another," I said, judging from the lines in his forehead he was old enough to know what a Mills bomb was. "And you are?"

"Constable Rutherford, sir."

"Did you hear what language this woman was speaking?"

"Could it have been French? Or possibly Eyetie?"

"*Français?*" I asked her. "*Italiano?*"

She stared blankly.

"Didn't think so. You come alone, Rutherford?"

"Yes, sir. I'm all Parkdale could spare till they knew what the situation was."

"The situation is I have to get this woman to medical attention, so you're taking over here. Call for what reinforcements you need. Notify HQ. Try to get a police photographer to record the position of the body. Don't let it be moved till he's done. I don't want guests from any of the rooms on this floor leaving the building till they've been identified and questioned. There's a young couple in number 26; the clerk will tell you which of the other rooms are rented out. Get him to open up the vacant ones too so you can sniff around. Then get everything you can out of the clerk himself. You there?"

"Me?" The clerk had a foolish Kaiser Wilhelm style moustache turned up at the corners of his mouth and a crusted-over cold sore on his upper lip.

"You rent a room to the man lying there? Don't look at his mouth; focus on his nose, eyes, forehead, hair, build."

The clerk looked at the corpse, then looked away and made a choking sound.

"All right, don't upchuck on my brogues. Go call me a taxi, then come back for another look. And don't let anyone check out of the hotel till they've seen me or this constable."

The Kaiser beat a retreat to the ground floor.

"While he's on the phone, Rutherford, you go through the deceased's pockets to see what we can learn about him. Now, miss. How about trying to sit up?"

I had no confidence that my words meant a thing to her, but my arm under her shoulders gave her the idea, and she managed it. Her expression was vacant, and her legs stuck straight out in front of her — an improvement on her previous posture even if now she looked more like a doll than ever. Relief made me smile. While her head was clearing, I took my first good, long look at her.

Her hair was dark, wavy, and medium short. An arrow-shaped nose ran straight and strong down the middle of an oval face to that arresting upper lip. Her arms and legs appeared capable and sturdy. There was nothing frail about her.

She looked, however, as if she'd been through it. Her complexion was rough, her cheeks deeply pitted. Dark circles, accentuated by her pallor, hung beneath those distant eyes. Creases bracketed her mouth. I had called her miss because she wore no jewellery on her ring finger, but she had evidently lived years beyond girlhood. Years without pampering. While I'm no expert on women's clothes, hers looked as if they'd been bought at deep discount from a department store basement. Her short-sleeved dress of thin, rust-coloured rayon had a fashionable low waist and sailor collar with matching tie, but was sloppily stitched at the shoulders. She wore no stockings, and her flimsy black T-strap shoes were mended with polish-blacked sticking plaster.

"What are you finding, Constable?" I asked over my shoulder.

The constable was plodding through every pocket of the deceased man's leatherette billfold. "Forty dollars and seventy-eight cents, sir."

"No driver's licence, passport, business cards, receipts, or train tickets? No scribbled notes of names, addresses, telephone numbers? No snaps of loved ones?"

"None of 'em."

"No army discharge papers? Looks like he could have used a refresher course in grenade throwing."

Rutherford held the empty wallet out to me. "See for yourself, sir."

"Get started on the other jobs then — and wish me better luck with the foreign lady's handbag."

"Think he meant to heave the egg over the transom, sir, and hung on too long?"

I looked above the door opening. A rectangular window, hinged along the bottom edge, stood open at a forty-five degree angle into the room. Evidently the glass had been sheltered from the blast and remained intact.

"That's as good a theory as any until we find out what *she* knows about it."

On the dresser in her room, I found a cloche hat in grey felt. Beneath it lay a small beaded hand-bag — containing only her room key and even less cash than the dead man's wallet. A twenty-four inch brown fibre suitcase stood in a corner. I was just about to try the catches when the case's owner made a protesting noise.

"So now your eyes are working," I said. "I call that progress."

Her first attempt to stand, however, was a no go, her foot slipping out from under her.

"Steady there," I scooped her up and deposited her in a cane-backed armchair. A who-are-you sounding question came from her in her own language. Or some language. I wasn't even sure she was speaking the same one each time. Sometimes I thought I heard a word of German emerging, but usually packed around with impenetrable sonic wool. "Do you understand Boche?" I ventured. "About all I can say is *Hände hoch!* — not too useful here. What's German for 'Sit quietly while I find out who you are'?"

She pointed to her suitcase and beckoned it towards her with both hands. Fearing too much upset might set her back, I stood the case beside her chair.

I saw no other personal effects in the small room. I found none in the wardrobe or in any drawers of the dresser. I looked under the bed, then between the mattress and spring, inside the pillow case, and through every fold of the bedclothes. I didn't rip open the pillow, but pinched it enough to satisfy myself no paper was hiding among the feathers. By then Rutherford was back to tell me our cab had arrived.

"Are you ready to try a little walking, miss?" I took the woman's arm, indicating that we were leaving. She shook her head and stayed seated.

"Look," I said. "You've had a bump on the head from a pretty heavy piece of lumber. You need to see a doctor. Now will you walk or shall I carry you?"

She sat staring, no longer vacantly, but right into my eyes. For the third time that morning, I hauled out my badge. She looked at it and back into my face. I was sure now she was catching on.

"We don't have bomb deaths in Toronto," I pushed on, "so there's going to be a fuss. You have no papers." I held her empty bag upside down. "If you won't go to the hospital, you'll have to come to the police station. Rutherford, show her your handcuffs."

The sight of them got her to her feet. Leaning on my arm, she walked slowly at first. She let me carry her suitcase. I persuaded her to hang on to the banister, and she got down the stairs all right. Rutherford remained behind with orders to keep everyone away from the mystery man's body while he checked the remaining rooms on the floor.

The lobby confirmed my first impression of a hotel on the downslope. By the window, a table covered in dog-eared magazines separated two low armchairs with stained upholstery. The white-panelled walls were in need of a fresh coat of paint while a leaf-bare stalk emerged from a handsome oriental plant pot. A bristol board sign on the desk read "Rooms $1.00"; the zeroes had been written on a square of notepaper pasted over a presumably higher number. I had to call the clerk out from a back recess. He smelled of schnapps. I got his name down as Frank Gabor.

"What language did this lady use when she checked in, Mr. Gabor?"

"I wouldn't know, sir. I go off duty at seven."

"The night clerk didn't say anything?"

Gabor shook his head.

"Russian, perhaps?"

"He didn't say."

"How many nights has she been here?"

"I'd have to look." Gabor made no move to do so.

I turned the register towards me. Opposite Room 29 for yesterday's date, September 2, was entered the name Lucy Clarkson. I didn't believe it for a moment, but at least I didn't have to call her Miss 29 anymore.

Chapter 2

LUCJA (LUCY) GRUDZINSKA, SO I heard later, was the wilful youngest child and only daughter of middle-class Warsaw parents. In a family of boys, she grew up outdoorsy and muscular, a contrast to her willowy mother and aunts. Since long before her birth, Russia had occupied that part of Poland — what had been Poland before the hard-luck country's neighbours carved it up between them. The Grudzinskis were Polish-speaking Catholics and wishful-thinking patriots. They stayed clear of political gatherings, however discreet, never dreaming of open disobedience to the Tsar's men. It drove Lucy up the wall having to listen to the might-have-beens, could-have-beens, should-have-beens voiced around the family dinner table. The comfort of their home made their laments all the more grating. No Grudzinski was going to bed hungry: perhaps foreign domination didn't gall her family as much as they pretended. Lucy herself wasn't the sort to complain and do nothing. She got involved with groups clamouring for reform and soon found herself arrested.

In an overcrowded holding cell at the Town Hall, she heard horror stories of Pavilion Ten at the Warsaw Citadel where the hardened "politicals" were sent, and was relieved to serve her thirty days in the gloomy but tolerable Pawiak Prison. Political inmates there — some nationalists, some Communists — found ways to communicate with each other and refine their thinking. Already infected by a poetic socialism, Lucy broadened her horizons. She became convinced that international peace and justice were goals more worthy of her idealistic energy than the narrower one of Polish autonomy. Tsarist oppression, she concluded, could be defeated only at its source. On her release from prison, she went to Russia to work for the Revolution brewing there.

Knowing what she wanted to learn, she learned fast. She mastered the Marxist line well enough to spread it. Eagerly, she absorbed and spoke the Russian of the Moscow workers. More at ease in the streets than in the parlour, she schooled herself to be tough, to care little what she ate, to not flinch at the sight of blood. Bit by bit, both before and after the Bolsheviks took power in 1917, Lucy — now calling herself Svetlana — earned the trust of her superiors. Despite her name change, she didn't have to hide her Polish origins. No one held them against her.

The proof of the confidence placed in her loyalty was the use Russia made of her in the 1920 war against

Poland. She accompanied the advancing army first as a translator, then as a spy or *swallow*. The Russian word meant not only a bird but also a secret service seductress. Training was necessarily brief. And luckily so, for sex with charmless functionaries was thought the way to desensitize a swallow to feelings of pleasure and romance. Lucy graduated with poor grades but untarnished ideals and went to work seducing Polish officers. She was too timid at first, but once she had "mastered her bourgeois scruples," she did wheedle out information of real, if limited, value. Along the way, she learned that all three of her brothers were fighting for Poland against Russia in Marshal Pilsudski's army, the very army she was working to undermine. But this news in no way shook her faith. She knew the Soviets came as liberators, not invaders. Pilsudski the defender of Poland? Eyewash, thought Lucy. The victory that — despite her best efforts — he ultimately won that summer was nothing but the Polish worker's defeat.

The failed Polish campaign was Lucy's initiation into a Soviet organization with a reputation so ugly that it had to keep changing its name. It had originally been the Cheka, later the GPU, and now OGPU — the Joint State Political Directorate. It's a name hard to take seriously in English: try saying *the feared OGPU* ten times quickly. But whatever they called themselves, they played rough. When the Red Army returned to Russia, Lucy's status was made official. She received specialized training and better rations. She learned the effect of ingesting various chemicals.

She learned how to kill with her bare hands. She was even issued a secret service uniform, which the nature of her duties meant she seldom wore.

I shake my head still when I think of all this. Of course, I flattered myself while I was walking Lucy Clarkson down the hotel stairs on that stinking hot September morning that as a good detective I was keeping an open mind about her history. But I was country miles from imagining the truth.

Late in 1921, she was sent to London to support the Communist Party of Great Britain's first baby steps. As a Pole, she aroused less suspicion than a Russian would have. Nonetheless, she found the assignment frustrating. She'd been given only minimal language training and, before she'd acquired any fluency in English, was whisked off to Germany. Here at least she knew the language, which she'd picked up as a girl.

During the negotiation of the 1922 Treaty of Rapallo, she was stationed in Berlin. Lucy's challenge this time, her biggest yet, was to obtain proof of what the Weimar Republic would ask of Bolshevist Russia and what concede in return. The work involved not only obtaining access to secret documents but photographing them and smuggling the film back to Moscow. Lucy was commended for her work and thought of herself as a successful discoverer of secrets — although she was to learn that the treaty finally ratified had unpublished military provisions she'd never even suspected. A side advantage of the Berlin posting was that one of her lovers there, a German diplomat formerly posted to the United

States, taught her to play poker. She bored easily when idle and loved the thrill of sudden gain. And if she lost, it was only money.

Not all Lucy's assignments were in foreign parts. Often she was set to work spying on Russians, particularly on the so-called specialists. Peasants and factory workers might be good Communists, but lacked — for example — engineering skills. It was conceded that for certain essential tasks non-proletarians had to be employed. Of course, their privileged class background meant they also had to be watched carefully. Lucy got good at assessing which specialist should be retained and which should be delivered to a secret service prison to be shot in the head.

She believed that she was building the world's first stable soviet state and that her contribution was recognized. When in 1922 membership in the Russian Communist Party topped 700,000, Lucy found herself in the elite two per cent that had fought in the underground before the Revolution. Then in 1924 Lenin died, and stability came into question. A short two years later, Trotsky's internationalism and Stalin's "socialism in one country" were duking it out for the party's soul.

In June 1926, Lucy was called to OGPU headquarters in Moscow's Dzerzhinsky Square. The agency was housed in an ornate, five-storey building called the Lubianka, home before the Revolution to an insurance company. Perhaps not too big a change of use, after all. OGPU insured Russia against damage by reactionaries. Lucy presented herself at the front door, in uniform for once. These uniforms had recently been simplified to remove sleeve insignia and badges of rank, which was now indicated only on the collar tabs. A sour porter, evidently weak-sighted, sent her to a side door. There she was met by a weedy official with greasy hair and a pistol on his belt. Instructed to follow him, she thought, *Suits me — I won't have to look at your scowling mug.* She followed him up broad staircases and down parquet-floored halls. Along one of the latter, a tall, broad-shouldered woman with a mole on her left cheek was approaching, stopping at one of a dozen similar doors. Lucy recognized someone she'd shared a shabby room with nearly ten years earlier and called the woman's name, which was Yulia Petrenko.

"Hey, Street Urchin," came the hearty reply. "You posted here?"

"Silence!" the escort bellowed, glaring at each woman in turn.

Lucy shook her head and pointed at Yulia, who pointed to the number on the door before disappearing behind it. The young man warned Lucy that he would have to report that she had engaged in forbidden conversation in the hall.

On ushering her into an oak-panelled office a moment later, he did just that. The grandmotherly woman behind the desk — a Georgian to judge by her name — dismissed him with a smile before telling Lucy to be seated. Comrade Beridze had pink cheeks, a large, sagging chest, and dust-grey hair pulled into a bun. Lucy had time to note these details in respectful silence while Comrade Beridze reviewed a dossier, into which she absent-mindedly sprinkled cigarette ash. Lucy asked if she too might smoke. Not getting an answer, she abstained. Eventually, Beridze started asking questions, ones designed to elicit any oppositionist leanings. Lucy took the line that she was a doer. She believed in the Revolution and approved anything the party leadership found necessary to protect it. Trotsky was at the time still a member of the Politburo, but unable to command a majority, so her answer was accepted. Beridze regretted the necessity of this examination: Comrade Grudzinska's record was exemplary. It was just that one of Lucy's superior officers had come under suspicion, and some thought that once rot was found in the branch, the twig couldn't be saved. Comrade Beridze disagreed. She believed she could count on Lucy. She would herself henceforth be responsible for assigning Lucy her duties and for receiving her reports.

Now Beridze set Comrade Grudzinska's dossier aside and squinted at a separate page of closely written notes. Lucy's next assignment would be to assess the reliability of Air Force Commander Arkadi Sergeievich Trigorin, inspector of military aircraft in the Voronezh region. Not a person Comrade Grudzinska could be expected to have heard of, so a word of introduction was in order. Before 1914, Trigorin had worked in the Russo-Baltic aircraft factory and during the war had flown bombers made by that company. After the Revolution, he'd been astute enough to join the Bolshevists. While not an aircraft designer, he knew as much about planes and flying as anyone in the

Red Army. For the past nine years his climb through the ranks had been steady, his loyalty unquestioned. Lately, however, murmurings had been heard that he had a weakness for women. Since his latest posting was particularly sensitive — in ways that Lucy need not concern herself with — OGPU had orders to set a reliable female agent to observe and test him. Lucy would be lent an air force identity and posted to Trigorin's office. Beridze told Lucy she would find Trigorin's file down the corridor in Room 3019. She was to read and commit it to memory.

"Here, Comrade," Beridze said, "take this pass authorizing you to enter the file room. You'll also appreciate, I think, that it permits you to walk in the halls unescorted. Hand it to one of the porters as you leave the building."

After studying the file as instructed, Lucy did not immediately leave the Lubianka. She tapped on the door of Room 3021, the door Yulia Petrenko had disappeared behind. Yulia welcomed her to what appeared to be an equipment depot. The furniture was a hodgepodge of bookshelves, dressers, buffets, china cabinets, and filing cabinets; anything that could be used for storage, whether cheaply knocked together at a people's furniture factory or liberated during the Revolution from an aristocrat's apartment. Behind glass doors could be seen Paris hats, pistols, and pill bottles. Lucy could only speculate as to what aids to espionage might be lurking in drawers, wardrobes, and cubby holes. The old pals chatted, then Yulia got Nikolai — her middle-aged co-worker — to take the two women's picture. Noticing the camera's resemblance to the one she'd used in Germany, Lucy asked to examine it. Yulia mischievously told her to keep it. It had been signed out to the hall-prowling snitch that had yelled at the two of them earlier. He'd wanted it to photograph an OGPU athletic event on the weekend, but he'd brought it back this morning with a few choice curses. He knew only about photographic plates and hadn't managed to thread the thirty-five millimetre film this "new toy" used. Comrade Petrenko had better have it loaded and ready for him before quitting time. In his indignation, this People's Hero had neglected to get a receipt, so officially he still had the camera. Quite a valuable one too, the latest from Germany. Yulia and Nikolai would happily swear he'd never brought it back.

Lucy had at that time no notion what use she might make of the camera. Taking it was just a prank. She knew she ran a risk of being searched as she exited the Lubianka, but seeing again her companion of the war years made her jaunty. She assumed an attitude of command with the sour porter, insisted he destroy her corridor pass before her eyes, and without interference left. By the front door.

Chapter 3

THE DESK PHONE WAS ringing as I guided the alleged Miss Clarkson out of the hotel towards the waiting cab. On seeing us, the driver jumped out and ran around to hold the door for us. Before we could get in, however, Rutherford was calling to me from the hotel entrance. I wasn't pleased to see him there.

"Constable?"

"Call for you, sir. An Inspector Sanderson at HQ insists on a word."

"Tell him I've left."

"Too late for that, sir, I'm afraid."

I knew a dozen constables that might have managed it, but this wasn't the time or place to argue. I told the cabbie to wait, shooed Rutherford back upstairs, and went to the phone.

"Shenstone here."

"Paul, I don't recall sending you to the Beaconsfield Hotel. What are you playing at?"

I reported everything I'd done since seeing the window explode. At first, Sanderson seemed more interested in why I had been coming in to work so late. The truth was I had been up most of the night trying to get a mad girl-child named Dot Perkins out of my room, but I wasn't about to go into that with the old puritan — even though I'd have been at my desk on time if I'd just given in to the imp. She was a shop assistant at the pharmacy where I bought my Aspirin. I'd made the mistake of giving her my address for delivery of some prescription medicine; now she thought she had a standing invitation to drop round whenever she craved male company.

I told Sanderson my alarm clock had failed to function. He said he'd be docking my pay — not a creative response, but no worse than my hackneyed excuse deserved. The ritual tut-tutting done with, the inspector said he wanted me to stay and direct the investigation. A police photographer was on his way.

"Let Rutherford handle that, sir. I've got to see to this woman's injuries."

"Constable Rutherford is not a detective, Paul. And I don't recall hearing that your illustrious war record involved service as a medic."

"I have had experience of how dangerous head wounds can be, and —"

"And I imagine your interest is all the greater when the wounded party is female."

My patience was thinning. "Inspector, a grenade fatality in a hotel corridor is going to be front page fodder right across the country, and the public will be howling for explanations. If I let this 'female' out of my sight, we may lose the one witness that can make sense of the incident."

Any reference to how the press would be exploiting a police story to the Toronto department's detriment was sure to raise Inspector Sanderson's blood pressure, but was a weapon with a high misfire rate. Instead of goading him on, it might make him dig in his heels — as he did now.

"Paul, you will get all you can from that crime scene and then come straight here to report to me in person. Is that understood?"

After assuring the inspector that I was not the one to have suffered a knock on the head, I sent Gabor to bring Rutherford down once more. I told the constable to take Miss Clarkson to the Toronto Western Hospital emergency department and not to lose track of her under any circumstances. I made sure he had the Beaconsfield Hotel phone number as well as Sanderson's. To Lucy's consternation, I retained her suitcase with me as I waved the cab and its two passengers off.

Before I could do anything with it, however, I was jostled from behind by someone in a hurry. Turning, I saw a face I knew. I had to look up to see it. Hastings MacDermid was a tall man with a tall head, and a lot of light brown hair on top of that. His newish summer suit and flatfoot straw hat looked a shade too stylish for the Beaconsfield.

"Hello, Hasty," I said. "Don't tell me you're registered here."

There were lines in his face the war hadn't put there, but his smile was as wide as ever and his wide, brown eyes just as humorous. When I'd first met him as a young lieutenant, just after my own commission came through, I'd made the mistake of asking him what the joke was. There wasn't one. He'd just been born sunny.

"Paul Shenstone! Isn't this a swell place? Put up at company expense for the whole run of the Exhibition. Golly, I've got to get down there. Why don't you come along and see my death-defying act?"

"Another time. Right now I'd like you to look at a body." It was a hell of a greeting, but I was glad to see him. Here was someone I could show a body to without fear of his throwing up. "I'm a cop," I added by way of apology.

"Doesn't surprise me a bit, PS. Always thought you'd be lost without the prospect of a scrap from time to time, not to mention the occasional whiff of danger. A body, eh? Lead on."

Hasty had been confident after the victory at Vimy Ridge that we'd have the war won by the end of 1917. All wrapped up, I'd replied, except for a little postscript of a year or two. That's when he'd started calling me by my initials.

I took him up to look at the bomb victim, already left too long unattended. I wasn't overjoyed to see Floyd once again standing over the remains, but he assured me that all he was doing was making sure they weren't interfered with. And, alone as I was, it was convenient to take him at his word.

Hasty took in the scene with a few more "gollies". He said he was sure he had never seen the deceased before. His room was at the back of the west end of the third floor. He thought he'd heard something vaguely explosive just before nine o'clock, but hadn't been particularly curious. His attention had been taken up cleaning the spots out of his suit (which I noticed was a spot-revealing silver grey) and massaging his bow tie into an approximation of symmetry. Since the bang wasn't repeated, he didn't investigate. He even wondered if his subconscious had thrown up a sound memory from the war years, although that sort of thing didn't tend to happen to him. Forward looking, that was Hasty Mac.

He told me he hadn't looked along the second-floor corridor as he came down the stairs from his third-floor room and so hadn't noticed the body; he'd been preoccupied with the fire extinguisher demonstrations he was contracted to do for the Conflagration Corporation. I described Lucy Clarkson of Room 29. Hasty said he'd never seen her either. Before I let him trot off to the Canadian National Exhibition grounds I got his assurance that he'd be coming back in the evening and staying at the Beaconsfield till the end of the holiday weekend.

"Then what?" I said. When I'd last seen him, seven years ago, he'd been full of the idea of using his discharge pay to enrol in some business college.

"Then it's off to another fall fair. The season's just beginning, so I've a couple of months to find something more long-term. Say, this case you've got on your hands looks pretty serious, but let's get together while I'm in town."

I said I'd drop by one evening.

"Splendid! You know, PS, it took me a moment to recognize you after all these years. Why'd you shave off your moustache?"

"It made me look too much like Ronald Colman," I said. "I was sick of folks asking for my autograph."

It was a eureka moment for Hasty. "Yes!" he exclaimed. "I can see that!"

How *do* you joke with someone that gullible?

When MacDermid had left, I found I was still carrying Miss Clarkson's suitcase. I tried the catches; they wouldn't move. The lock would have been easy enough to force, but I didn't like to do so until I'd had another chance to speak to the owner. Besides, I had enough to keep myself out of trouble. I had Kaiser Frank lock the case in the hotel safe and write me a receipt.

The police photographer and another constable showed up, which made life a lot easier. I was even happier to welcome onto the scene a fresh-faced, fair-haired acting detective named Ned Cruickshank. I'd worked with him before and found him wet behind the ears, but keen. On his own initiative, he'd brought a fingerprinting kit.

By the end of the morning, this is what we had.

A dozen of the Beaconsfield's twenty guest rooms had been rented out the night before, six on the second floor and six on the third. Occupants of two of these twelve rooms were reported to have checked out during Frank Gabor's first hour of work today, between seven and eight. Among the vacancies were Room 27, the one next to Lucy Clarkson's, and number 28, the room across the hall from hers, as well as the two on each floor with private baths, rooms that rented for sixty cents more a night. None of the eight vacant rooms contained anything beyond standard hotel furnishings. On each floor was located a shared bath and separate water closet for the rooms without facilities of their own. These showed signs of a day's normal use, nothing out of the ordinary.

None of the guests we spoke to that morning recognized the deceased. The nearest occupied room was number 26, that of Jenny and Floyd Peters of Waterloo, Ontario. He was a railway telegrapher. Until their marriage in April, she had clerked in a dry goods shop. They were in town to visit the Canadian National Exhibition, too long after the wedding for it to feel like a honeymoon, but their first trip together nonetheless. Isabella Lang, the elderly by-the-month resident of Room 22, was still asleep when we knocked. Like the hotel itself, she had plainly seen better times. There was a rip in the armpit of the silk kimono in which she came to the door. A bottle of invalid port stood on her dresser beside a silver tea service. Her window was closed despite the heat, and the odour of toilet water hung heavy in the confined space. She said she'd been wakened by something like an explosion, but had dropped off again immediately. It was such a noisy hotel, being right on Queen Street, that she couldn't afford to pay attention to every bang and pop. On the other hand, a Belgian tourist by the name of Pierre Leclercq said he had looked out the door of his room, number 23, when he heard the bomb. He'd observed one man standing over the body of another and judged it prudent to lie low. He said he knew nothing more about the incident, so I let him bustle off to see the less gruesome Toronto sights. He wanted to take in a real skyscraper and had read that the tallest building in the British Empire, all twenty storeys of it, was to be found on the northeast corner of King and Yonge Streets.

I was told that six of the guest rooms — including Hasty's — were rented to parties not currently occupying them. Frank Gabor finally pulled himself together enough to have a proper look at the body, now waiting for an ambulance to take it to Grace Hospital for autopsy. The nervous hotel clerk swore that the deceased wasn't Gladys Crew, the journalist from Room 32. This was a start. Nor, he asserted with gathering courage, was the bomb victim anyone he'd seen before. Not the Italian businessman Leo Di Giovanni from Room 38. Certainly not Room 24's Bartholomew Rogers, who had mentioned that he'd been taken on by a local boat builder and was living in the hotel while he looked for an apartment in the neighbourhood. Mr. Rogers had been seen to leave for work before the blast. On the other hand, Gabor had never set eyes on Room 33's Dan Ewart, listed in the register as unemployed, or on the couple in Room 25. Their name was recorded as Pollard and they had a rural route home address. These three people had checked in and presumably gone out between seven p.m. and seven a.m., when Gabor's overnight counter-part Alex Horvath was on duty.

I asked Gabor whether anyone could have entered or left the hotel after 7 seven without his knowledge. He said not by the front door, at least not this morning. He hadn't left the desk. I called him on that. All right, he said, but he hadn't been away for more than thirty seconds. Not even a call of nature since coming on duty. There was also the back door by which the cleaning woman had arrived. It required a key to open from the outside. As far as Gabor knew, there were only three keys: the one Marija Babic held, one held in the office behind the front desk, and one in the possession of the owner-manager, Mr. Ferraro, who seldom visited the premises. On the exterior wall of the west end of the building, there was a fire escape, accessed by windows in the second- and third-floor corridors.

Ned and I went upstairs to have a look. The two windows were held closed by catches on the inside, but would not trigger a fire alarm if opened. Ned brushed all the catches for prints, but none came up. I did, however, find a deposit of black soot on the hall floor inside the third-floor access window. Soot very like that which my fingers picked up when I ran them along the slats of the escape's top landing just outside. The fire escape was the standard open-work steel structure, painted black, with passage from the third floor to the second by metal stairs and from the second to the ground by a metal ladder on tracks. Counterweights kept the ladder up when not needed.

When I stepped onto it, it rolled — with less clatter than a passing streetcar — down its tracks. Once I reached the ground and got off, the weights lifted the ladder out of reach again.

I had a look from outside, front and back, at the one-storey butcher shop on the hotel's east side. I saw no way up to the flat, tarred roof. The butcher told me that the only access would be by ladder, and that he didn't keep one on the premises. I went back into the Beaconsfield by the front door and up to the broken window at the east end of the second floor. From there, I had a look down at the butcher's tarred roof, glistening with glass shards. I put the drop from sill to roof at seven feet. Unless he'd been an acrobat, the small, dead man would have had a hard time getting into the hotel that way. Also, anyone on the south side of Queen could have seen him propelling himself in through that window. I sent a man to check. None of the south-side shopkeepers had seen anything of the kind.

When we'd finished with Gabor and the guests, I had a word with Marija Babic. She was a squat, square woman of about forty. A few wisps of brown hair showed from under the red cloth she'd fashioned into a turban. She said the back door had been closed and locked as usual when she arrived. I hadn't intended to make her look at the body, but something about her convinced me she could take it. She stood studying the damaged face with her hands in the pockets of her blue checked smock. She was sure she had never seen the man before. I took down her address and told her that she was not to clean any of the rooms today. In fact, she could let me have her pass key. She handed it over, luckily without asking to see a warrant. Her only question was whether she could now go home.

I didn't have the authority to close the Beaconsfield and, frankly, didn't see any point in doing so. But if the hotel were to remain open for business, the bloodstains on the hall floor had to be cleaned up and the window patched or fixed. We had photographs of both; they would have to do. I instructed Mrs. Babic to clean the baths and WCs as usual and put special effort into sweeping and scrubbing the floorboards of the second-floor corridor. She snorted something sarcastic, presumably in Serbian, and stumped off to pick up her kit.

Ned Cruickshank passed her in the hall. "The stretcher party's here, Sergeant. Shall I let them take the body?"

"Tell them there's to be no dissection until the night clerk Alex Horvath has had a look at him. Better yet, phone the pathologist and tell him. Then get Horvath down there. Mr. Gabor should have his address. With any luck he'll be asleep in his bed by now and easy to find."

"And delighted to see me," Cruickshank said ruefully.

"If you wanted to be popular, Ned, you chose the wrong line of work. Here, hang on a minute. Before we lose sight of this bird, let's see where his clothes come from. Check the insides of his shoes; I'll take the messy end."

Rigour had set in, and I could see Cruickshank's pink cheeks getting pinker with the effort as he wiggled the deceased's left shoe back and forth. Although the acting detective's suit was still new, dating from his recent promotion out of uniform, he was kneeling on the dirt-tracked floor, not trying to do his job from a fastidious crouch.

"Take your time, Ned," I advised. "Loosen the laces a bit more. Hang on now."

The shoe slipped out of his grasp as the body shifted position. I was lifting the deceased's shoulders to get a look inside the back of his jacket. The movement stirred up the smell of blood that was developing nicely in the heat. Cruickshank cleared his throat.

"Bata shoes."

"Wear them myself," I said. "Made in Europe, exported everywhere. I don't think we can make much of that. Any soot on the soles?"

Cruickshank gave them a rub and showed me his fingers.

"Any black particles like that on your own shoes?"

He checked and said not.

"Then I'm guessing one of the hotel guests unfastened a window, being careful not to leave fingerprints on the catches, and let our bomber come up the fire escape. Aha, the tag inside his collar has a red star on it. Ever seen one of those?"

"Not in a jacket. Is it from Russia, do you think?"

"Macy's."

When Ned Cruickshank had left to rouse the night clerk, I used Marija Babic's pass key to have a preliminary look at the rooms of the guests that had left for the day. It wasn't to be a thorough search as I had no warrants — and on present evidence no hope of getting any. I just wanted to see if I could narrow the field of suspects.

Isabella Lang remained in her room and I didn't disturb her. I discovered that Bartholomew Rogers had by his bedside a book about Italy under Mussolini. For his part, Dan Ewart had in the bottom of his wardrobe a pile of leaflets on the subject of "Socialism in one country," that country being the Soviet Union. Not likely to become a Book of the Month Club selection any time soon, I figured. All the same, I picked up a copy for bedtime reading. The Beaconsfield Hotel was turning out to be more international than the League of Nations.

There were no surprises in the next few rooms. Leaflets from the exhibition strewn around Floyd and Jenny's bower, especially ones from the auto show featuring the new, improved cars of the coming year. Maps of North America on Pierre Leclercq's dresser. A neat row of male toiletries on Leo Di Giovanni's. Two peaches and three apples on the Pollards' window sill. What caught me up short was Room 32, Gladys Crew's. There was nothing there: no clothes, no grooming aids, nothing to eat, and no reading material — except for a copy of Ewart's pamphlet in the waste basket. I wondered if the newswoman had slipped out without paying. Not so, however. When I got Gabor to show me the register, I saw he'd simply neglected to tell me she'd left, having squared her account and returned her key in the proper form at 8:30 that morning.

I next phoned Grace Hospital. They had the body, but Cruickshank and Horvath had not yet arrived. I instructed the pathologist's assistant to send the deceased's clothes to Dalton Linacre, the chemistry professor at the University of Toronto, with instructions to analyze any powder residue found and see if he could tell us more about the bomb.

Gabor was hanging around the phone listening to my end of the conversation.

"Anything more you'd like to tell me?" I asked him.

"No, nothing."

"You think of anything, remember anything, hear anything, see anything, phone this number." I wrote it out for him. I should have had business cards, but the city was on one of its economizing binges — stopping just short of acting on Mayor Thomas Foster's suggestion that it would be cheaper to reimburse robbery victims from public funds than to hire police. My name and number didn't take up a whole page of my department-issued notebook, so I gave Gabor only the bottom half. "Otherwise," I went on, "business as usual. Don't talk about the case with anyone. Now let's have that suitcase from the safe."

He got it for me, a little unsteadily.

"I could use a drink for the road as well."

"I don't —"

"Skip it, Frank. You've been tippling all morning."

He straightened his tie. "I was going to say I don't have a glass." There was malice in his smile.

"Let's have the bottle then." I could have had him fetch me a glass from one of the guest rooms, but I was ready to go, and there was no pus actually flowing from the swelling on his lip. I poured a generous ounce of plum brandy into my mouth and swallowed it down. My chaser was a cone of fish and chips from the shop across the alley from the hotel. I took the opportunity of asking the proprietor if he'd noticed anything around the time of the blast, but he hadn't arrived at his shop till 9:30. An eastbound streetcar was coming, so I didn't probe further. I jumped aboard with lunch in one hand and Lucy's case in the other.

Chapter 4

WHEN COMMANDER ARKADI TRIGORIN noticed the new woman assigned to his office, he expected she'd been sent to spy on him and said she should go right ahead: the only woman he feared was his wife Olga.

Lucy had come the three hundred miles from Moscow by train. It was her first time in the southern Russian city of Voronezh, which at 120,000 was big enough to have a ballet-opera theatre. She soon learned that Trigorin liked going backstage to offer homages to the young sopranos and ballerinas, but also that his visits were short and — by all reports — correct. Lucky for the slender, delicate-skinned girls he favoured, as he himself was thick and hard at every point. Thick arms, broad in the chest, a thick neck. The back of his head dropped straight to his collar, and there was little over-hang to his chin. His moustache was thick and black.

Of the women in the air inspectorate office, his favourite appeared to be a fragile blonde perpetually in tears at the thought she might have done something wrong. Trigorin would pat Nina's shoulder and whisper in her ear while she stared helplessly at her typewriter keyboard. You had to wonder why she was there. Once again, though, Lucy could discover no evidence of more going on between the two than everyone in the office could see.

Then, out of the blue — it was the Friday before midsummer — Trigorin told Lucy she would be accompanying him to Lipetsk, which she knew from her paper-pushing as home to the 4th Squadron of the Red Air Force. She had half an hour to pack an overnight bag. He would meet her at his plane.

Never having flown before, Lucy approached the two-seater warily. It was about twenty-four feet long, painted olive green with a red star on its tail. Unlike the canvas-covered wooden biplanes of the war era, it was all metal and had only one wing, held above the body on struts — what Trigorin called a parasol configuration. Asked the make of this improbable device, he called it a Junkers Ju-21. A German plane then, said Lucy. No, Trigorin insisted indignantly, a Russian plane.

Wondering if that news should be reassuring, Lucy climbed into the rear seat, which was elevated slightly compared to Trigorin's in front. After takeoff, the commander piloted his Junkers sixty-five miles north by northeast along the Voronezh River. Lucy had been given goggles, but there was no canopy or windshield and she took a sporty pleasure in the stinging breeze on her face. She pretended to enjoy also the steep climbs and tight turns Trigorin did to scare her. When they started to descend, she saw that the Lipetsk base consisted of about twenty buildings and two runways. Trigorin could have used both runways laid end to end, he landed at such terrific speed. Lucy believed they would end up in the bushes and wasn't wrong by more than a foot or two.

She'd been on the ground barely long enough to catch her breath before she realized that the planes she'd seen parked at the perimeter of the field were Great War derelicts that would never fly again. And the airmen that came to greet her, while they wore Russian uniforms, were as Slavic as the Kaiser. Plainly the 4th Squadron of the Red Air Force existed only on paper. Trigorin made it clear she needn't expect him to answer her questions. He'd brought her this far from Voronezh and Olga for another reason, which he made clear as soon as he got her to the two-room cabin reserved for his personal use.

She was prepared for some advance, and for it to be coarse, but not for the urgency of Trigorin's appetites, which made his every touch bruising. Lucy smouldered with rage. To use sex to further the Revolution, yes, she was prepared for that; but to submit to this mauling was no work for an OGPU agent. At least she had the answer to Comrade Beridze's question. She could in theory have put Trigorin under immediate arrest. In theory. But she didn't know whether there was anyone on the base she could count on to back her up. In OGPU terms, she suspected, she wasn't even supposed to be here. There was some secret about Lipetsk — perhaps the secret that made Trigorin's job particularly sensitive, but that Lucy wasn't authorized to know. Before she put up any resistance to the commander, she had to find out the lay of the land. Curiosity and caution made her choke back her anger and swallow her humiliation.

Her repugnance was nothing to Trigorin; it neither aroused nor offended him. He simply didn't trouble to notice it and would not, Lucy believed, have recognized what he was doing as rape.

Afterwards, he entertained her with cigarettes and vodka and his flying anecdotes. He had convinced himself that she would look forward to many repetitions of his attentions over the next two or three days. After the first attack, she was at least prepared; she even found ways to make the encounters less painful. And she kept her eyes open, building a picture of what really went on at Lipetsk. It was a flying school for the German military and a facility where the latest warplanes could be test flown. These machines were never left parked by the runway, but kept out of sight in hangars. There were Junkers monoplanes like Trigorin's made at the town of Fili, outside Moscow. The best fighter planes, however, were Fokkers imported from Holland. These were said to be more powerful, better climbers, bigger, and faster than anything Britain or the United States could command. Germany was building a forbidden air force outside her borders and out of sight of the allied control commissions. In exchange, the Russian hosts got modern planes for their own air force and training in German military science.

So much Lucy gathered by eavesdropping on conversations in German, which she was believed not to understand, and by conversations with any German pilots themselves that spoke some Russian. They were sworn to secrecy, of course, but from her air force uniform they inferred she was in on the secret. And their enjoyment of what they were doing made them talkative, if not boastful. Flying and high spirits seemed to go together.

On her second day in Lipetsk, Lucy had an opportunity to hear more. Trigorin had finished what he thought of as lovemaking and, while Lucy was pretending to sleep, he entertained the senior German in the next room. The rough plank partition had been knocked together with no thought of soundproofing. Lucy pressed her ear to a knothole. She understood only some of what Trigorin said: whether from regard for security or for her supposed slumbers, he kept his voice low — and his German was heavily accented. Trigorin's guest, on the other hand, spoke as fearlessly and confidently as the pilots he commanded. *His* voice was clear and ringing, although both drinkers got louder as the vodka flowed. They called each other Volker and Arkadi. It became a great game for these Great War enemies to plan the coming war on Poland. This project sounded to Lucy not at all like the Soviet campaign to liberate the Polish worker of 1920. The jolly chatter had a very different drift.

"Poland is intolerable," said Volker. "It must be destroyed."

"Drink," said Arkadi, "drink to the boundaries of 1914. Russia and Germany sharing a frontier of sixteen hundred kilometres, with no buffer states between. Plague on buffer states."

"A common border, yes," said Volker, "but straighter than in 'fourteen. Between our land and yours, my friend, a thousand kilometres would be long enough."

"France won't be able to save Poland," Arkadi proclaimed.

"England won't lift a finger."

"England will be Bolshevik."

"Whoa, friend," said Volker, still loud but calming. "None of that Bolshevism for export. Export your vodka and keep the Bolshevism for your own people. You can have Bolshevism in your share of Poland."

"The hell with politics," said Arkadi. "Drink to flying, drink to dropping bombs on the Poles. Big bombs. Little bombs. Gas bombs. Drop enough bombs and it won't matter if the corpses are capitalist or Communist."

Lucy knew that these commissioned blowhards, big enough frogs in their own ponds, swam far below the circles of power where policy was set. Their exchanges could be dismissed as boozy vapourings without authoritative backing; all the same, they filled her with such fury that keeping still was torment.

From her listening post, she heard the officers' conversation take a technical turn. Soon after, the two left the building to test the tuning of the engine in Volker's plane. Lucy seized the opportunity to have a good snoop around Trigorin's premises. He was not as a rule careless with documents. His desk and safe were always kept locked. His Florentine leather briefcase, however, was old — a pre-Revolutionary relic. A metal plate crimped to the end of the leather strap carried a staple that clicked into the lock. This plate was loose. Perhaps the case was the gift of a family member or former lover, and some unwise sentiment prevented Trigorin from replacing it. Lucy took advantage of his lapse.

She found an inventory of the airplanes that had passed through the Lipetsk facility, along with their technical specifications. In the margins and on the reverse of these papers, Trigorin had noted by hand how the machines had behaved in test flights. There was also a memo on future Russo-German aviachemical tests to ascertain the feasibility of spraying mustard gas from planes onto enemy ground troops. Among these papers, Lucy discovered a letter. It was dated Tuesday, May 11, 1926, and was on the letterhead of the Chief Directorate of the Air Force of the Red Army, Commissariat of Military and Naval Affairs. It was addressed to Commander A. S. Trigorin, Inspectorate of Aircraft, District G, Voronezh, Russian SSR.

Outside the sun was shining. Sparrows were chirping in the eaves of the cabin. Then the revving up of a twelve-cylinder Napier Lion engine silenced or drowned out the birdsong — and, a moment later, just as effectively, the pounding of blood in Lucy's ears obliterated the engine's roar. The paper trembled in her hand so that the Russian words danced before her eyes. At the same time, those words appeared to be typed much larger than they were and lit by a light brighter than the sunbeams pouring through the western window.

This letter shifted the centre of Lucy's universe. Suddenly, the ground beneath her feet was in motion. The ideological concrete with which she had paved over her love of her native land was blown sky-high; the world revolution to which she had given her heart had become a narrow nationalism, land-greedy, calculating, homicidal. The scourge of capitalism and imperialism? No more. Well, she would have no more of it. She was only one voice of protest, but if the Russo-German pact was vulnerable through its secrets, she would use those secrets to destroy it.

She needed proof. She had the camera in her overnight bag, but it was too dangerous to start snapping the documents now. Trigorin might be back at any moment. She couldn't make copies after he went to bed tonight: there wouldn't be enough light. Her best chance was early morning, before the commander was awake. This morning, he had not opened his eyes till six, when the sun was already high in the sky. Promising, but one morning was not enough to set a pattern, and Lucy couldn't wait for the evidence of other mornings. She decided to take out some insurance.

That evening she slipped the contents of two veronal capsules into Trigorin's nightcap. She washed his glass as soon as he dozed off. The last thing she wanted was for him to wake up groggy and wonder what the white residue was. At four thirty a.m., she took Trigorin's briefcase and Yulia's Leica into the bushes that surrounded the airfield. She spread her tunic on the ground, placed the papers on it one by one, and weighted each page down with twigs and coins. Luckily there was no breath of wind.

She took her pictures and got everything back in place, including herself back to bed, before Trigorin woke. He woke with no suspicion he'd been drugged, but out of sorts all the same. He found dew on Lucy's boots and accused her of having sneaked out early to meet one of the Germans. She replied that she'd been sleepless and had just gone for a walk alone; she'd seen no one. Unconvinced, Trigorin struck her in the face, breaking a tooth. Lucy hoped his jealousy would occasion a speedy return to Voronezh, but they stayed on another miserable day, during which Lucy found herself imprisoned in Trigorin's bedroom and at the mercy of his amorous whims.

Next morning the commander was awake early, feigning sleep in the hopes he'd catch Lucy attempting another early-morning tryst. When she didn't stir, he got up stealthily — remarkably so considering his habitual brutishness — with the intention of searching her overnight bag. Lucy leaped from the bed. "Let me help you with that, Comrade," she said. "Is this what you're looking for?" She reached into her bag. When her hand came out, it was holding her OGPU badge. She told him he needn't look so disconcerted. He'd always suspected, hadn't he? In any case, there was no cause for alarm. In view of the pleasure they'd taken together, she could overlook much in his conduct, his jealousy included. Even his smashing her in the mouth she could interpret as a flattering sign of his deep feelings. But he had no authorization to inspect her bag, and if he did so she would arrange accommodation for him in the basement of the Lubianka. There one had no need of an overnight bag as there were enough prisoners shot each day to furnish the survivors with serviceable clothes — once the ones they arrived in had fallen to rags. Trigorin blustered that no secret servicewoman would behave as she had done. Fine, she replied coolly. He could put her assertion of authority to the test. If he were a true modern Russian, she said, he would comply with orders, however absurd, however improbable their source. Or her favourite pilot could gamble his specialist's reputation on disobedience and risk burial in a cell so deep he'd never again see the sky.

Trigorin's idea of saving face was flying Lucy back to Voronezh without breakfast, which annoyed her not a bit. She couldn't get done with him fast enough. In the privacy of her own cockpit in his plane, she breathed more freely. Once landed, she asked to be excused from the office that day. Trigorin grunted permission.

On reaching her quarters, she changed from her air force to her OGPU uniform, which would obtain her more deference from the petty officials she'd encounter between Voronezh and the frontier. Many of these, drawn from the level of society worst off before the Revolution, would be illiterate — better able to read a secret service black-buttoned tunic and blue forage cap than the travel pass she lacked. That lack would be fatal on the better policed highways and railways, so Lucy's journey west would have to be by the slowest and roughest back roads. By plane it would have been no more than eight hundred miles west to Warsaw, only twice the range of one of those wonderful Fokker D.XIII fighters. Lucy was looking at a much longer trek.

In Kursk she sold the camera. She didn't need the money quite this soon, but reasoned that it would fetch a better price in a larger town. She spent the proceeds frugally, delaying as long as possible the necessity of commandeering the peasants' food. Hitching rides on wagons and in vans, she came in late July to the heavily patrolled border area. From here she had to walk and then crawl into Poland with no more than the film and the clothes she had on.

She was under no illusions that the Pilsudski dictatorship was about to welcome her home. The photographs she'd carried so far were more likely to be dismissed as the trick of a spy and traitor than accepted as the bona fides of a born-again Pole. Her plan was to contact first her brother Piotr, the sibling she had been closest to in age and temperament. The two of them had raced bicycles side by side down steep country lanes over loose gravel, reckless as to the oncoming lorry around the next blind corner. She wondered if Piotr had fulfilled his ambition to study engineering. If so, he'd be able to appreciate the technical data she'd collected regarding the aircraft being marshalled against Poland.

Meanwhile, though, she had to acquire civvies and get to Warsaw. She had no remaining roubles, which would in any case have done her more harm than good. She had no Polish marks, which in any case Poland had not used since their catastrophic devaluation three years earlier. She had no zlotys, the replacement currency, which she had never seen. Crime, Lucy felt, was her only option.

Outlawry was not new to her, of course; all her work in Russia before the Revolution had been in Tsarist terms illegal. Just as her theft of Trigorin's documents and subsequent escape from Russia had been illegal in Soviet terms. But what she had to do to survive now was different. For the first time she would be breaking the laws of a society with which she was *not* at war. She reminded herself that whatever enabled her warnings to be heard was ultimately for Poland's good. Still, she felt she was about to bite into a pretty wormy apple.

She braced herself and bit. Her first theft was of the clothes of a village dairymaid she waylaid at dusk. Lucy grabbed the girl's throat and squeezed till she passed out.

Using a combination of theft — with or without violence — and seduction, she reached Warsaw on the last day of July. Some of the people she stole from along the way were already struggling to put food on their tables, and for making them poorer she was sorry. At least, she made sure she left no one destitute.

As she approached her native city, she tried to work out how she was going to get a message to Piotr. Even if her family didn't know the treacherous part she'd played in the 1920 war, she had left against their wishes. A letter to her brother at the old address might be read by unfriendly eyes. She wrote instead to a former schoolmate who'd lived in the same New Town apartment block as the Grudzinskis. The two girls had been friends and athletic rivals, dividing between them the honours in track and field. Lucy didn't know if any members of Wanda's family could still be reached there, but didn't want to call in person for fear of meeting one of her own parents or brothers. In fact, she shrank from showing her face on Freta Street at all and suggested meeting Wanda at noon two days hence at the Copernicus Monument in the Old Town. She hoped Wanda would appreciate her choice of the astronomer's statue as a symbol of Polish nationalism. In the old days, Lucy had disapproved of what she'd seen as Wanda's political narrowness. She'd gone to Russia without telling her friend goodbye.

Lucy arrived ten minutes late in front of the Staszic Palace, which she barely recognized. Since Poland had regained her independence, the building had sloughed off all false and gaudy Russian decoration, leaving uncovered for the first time since Lucy's birth its original, clean-lined face. Lucy was too preoccupied to investigate what lay behind the dressed white stone and classical columns, but hoped some scientific inquiry — suppressed by the Russians — was now flourishing there.

She studied every woman that passed through the busy square. Most were too short or too old. None approached her. By 12:20, she began to despair of the reunion with Wanda, and stayed twenty minutes more only because she could think of nowhere else to go. Then a pale, serious woman with a long stride detached herself from the crowd and made for where Lucy stood in the shadow of the statue. The expression on Wanda's long face was grim, whether from animosity or sorrow Lucy could not say — until Wanda's strong arms looped around her in an embrace so fiercely warm it took Lucy's breath away. Wanda wasn't angry. Her news, however, was bad.

Her parents knew how things stood with their neighbours the Grudzinskis. Piotr had been killed in the Russo-Polish War; Lucy's father had suffered a stroke. Her two surviving brothers had disowned her.

Lucy did not attempt to go home. Instead, she concentrated on delivering her warning of the new conspiracy to wipe her country off the map. It promised well that Wanda was now married to the secretary of the Polish Olympic Committee with acquaintances in the Ministry of Foreign Affairs. Following these leads, Lucy caught the interest of a junior government official named Jan Tomczak. Unfortunately, Jan was more interested in a fling than in introducing her to his superiors. If she had evidence that Russia and Germany were plotting Poland's destruction, he said, it would be wasted in Warsaw. The government already believed in the threat; the trick was to convince the Versailles victors that their peace treaty needed enforcing.

It may have been that, after a few hot dates, Don Juan was giving Lucy the brush-off, but she accepted his advice to take her discoveries to London. It didn't hurt that Jan was offering not only to cover travel expenses but also to arrange travel documents. Leaving town appealed to her even more after she was almost run down in front of the Jablkowski department store by a car containing two grim-faced men. She suspected the long arm of OGPU.

By this time she'd had her film developed. Photos of one document were too poorly focused to read, even when the prints were magnified to poster size, but the crucial letter was clear and intact.

Chapter 5

MY THOUGHT WAS TO relieve Constable Rutherford at Lucy's bedside. When I got off the car at Bathurst, I squinted towards the lake into the blazing midday sun and could see no northbound to transfer onto. So I dropped the greasy newspaper that had contained my chips in a trash bin, slung my suit jacket over my shoulder, and walked the five blocks up to the Western Hospital.

Behind a broad strip of parched lawn on the east side of Bathurst, the long, red-brick building went up three storeys on top of a high basement. The pile wasn't old, but dated from before the war, so money had been spent on turrets and pillars and decorated corners. It wasn't my money so I didn't mind. That was outside. Inside, by contrast, it was all business in the fight against germs. I was immediately sobered by the starkness of unending white — white paint on the walls, white tiles on the floors, white enamel desks, white sheets and blankets, high white collars on the nurses' white dresses. The eye's only relief was the occasional gleam of aluminum on a food wagon or the black rubber of the tires on which stretchers rolled noiselessly down snowy corridors. I've nothing against white, and I guess the look of cleanliness reassures surgery patients, but I hoped Miss Clarkson didn't require surroundings quite so monochrome.

The sterile tranquility of the Western made me think back to the military hospitals where the stench of putrefaction filled your nose and horrors met your eye at every turn. Volunteer nurses had had to make up with human warmth for their lack of spotless uniforms and years of training. They hadn't had time to learn not to flirt, whereas these impassive vestals ... Just then one passing me returned my smile with twinkling eyes, and I felt better about the human race.

The feeling didn't last. I was looking for an information desk when I saw with dismay Constable Rutherford push his way in through the street doors.

"Where's the patient?" I asked.

The constable didn't answer at once. He seemed to be trying to work loose with his tongue some morsel of food stuck between his teeth.

"Having a nap when I left her, sir," he said at last.

"Show me."

The constable led the way up a grand stairway into a rectangular, high-ceilinged room on the second floor. Tall windows lined the long walls, and beneath each row of windows ran a row of white-enamelled beds, most of them occupied. The women were either sitting up reading or knitting, or else lying down sleeping or moaning. The moaning was soft as nurses moved about the ward soothing and shushing. I saw no visitors, this apparently being a quiet time. Around each bed ran a curtain track, but most of the white cotton curtains were pushed back against the wall, so the beds and their occupants could be seen. Rutherford was leading me towards one of the exceptional screened-off beds.

I hadn't liked it that Rutherford had let Lucy out of his sight, and I didn't like it that I still couldn't see her. But I was just prepared to entertain the possibility that a doctor was giving her some privacy while he examined her. Prepared, that is, until I noticed that the snap was open on the leather pouch on the right side of Rutherford's belt. I tugged his sleeve.

"Constable, where're your nippers?"

His hand went into the pouch and came out empty. When he looked at me, I thought I'd never seen such a foolish face on a grown man.

Inside the curtain, we found the handcuffs around the slender wrists of a frightened-looking fair-haired girl. She lay flat on her back with the bedclothes pulled up to her chin, her bare arms above her head. The sides of her nose bore the indentations of spectacles, which she was not wearing. The chain between her wrists had been passed around a vertical bar in the bed frame. Beside her, one hand on the girl's shoulder, stood a nurse with early grey in her hair, a squarish face, and large, brown eyes.

"There, Benny," said the latter. "The constable's back with his key."

You'd think from the woman's calm that people in her ward got chained to beds every day.

"Quietly now, sirs," she went on. "We don't want to alarm the patients."

"How long since she got away?" was my first, urgent question.

"Hours," said the fettered girl with feeling — to be corrected promptly by her cool-headed companion.

"I didn't see her leave, but it can't have been more than fifteen minutes. Or less than ten."

More than enough time for a vanishing act.

"I'm sure it felt longer," I said, mild as milk.

After some fumbling in his uniform trouser pockets, Rutherford found the key and got the cuffs off the girl. He was about to put them back into their pouch.

"I'll take those, constable," I said. Our eyes met. "The key too." I lifted cuffs and key out of his hand and stowed them in an inside pocket of my suit jacket.

The brown-eyed nurse was examining each of the girl's wrists.

"Just a little redness, Ben. No break in the skin. Now I know you policemen will want to ask Nurse Bennett all about what happened." She turned to me. "I assume you're police as well. You can both wait in the nurses' day room while we get some clothes on her. That's the room with the bay window when you turn left at the far end of the ward."

"You'd better come as well," I said.

I got her name, which was Jane Sparrow. The other was D. Bennett — D. for Daisy. She hated the name, so no one called her that.

However swell the day room might be for an interview, I wasn't about to lose track of any more witnesses, so Rutherford and I hung about the ward until the curtain around Lucy's bed was pulled back and the two women emerged. Meanwhile, to each patient's inquiry as to what was going on, I smiled sweetly and — dropping my voice to the most confidential level — replied, "It's an investigation. Nothing to be alarmed about."

Inside ten minutes, Nurses Sparrow and Bennett were sitting with Rutherford and myself in a room that daringly departed from the hospital's universal whiteness. The walls were painted a mother-of-pearl grey and the armchairs were upholstered in a utilitarian buff. Miss Bennett was wearing a nurse's dress pinned up at the hem, and three sizes too ample for her slender figure. Her own uniform — dress, cap, apron, and shoes, but *not* her stockings — had been taken by the "patient" whose fretful noises had summoned her into the curtained cubicle. Once there, she explained — with an understandable sense of grievance in her voice, but also with a woman-of-science matter-of-factness — she had been grabbed by the neck and had pressure applied to her carotid arteries until an interrupted flow of blood to the brain had caused her to faint. When she came to, she had found herself covered only with a bedsheet and chained to the head of the bed, while her sturdy white stockings had been used to tie her ankles to the bed frame at the other end. A hospital nightie had been tied around her mouth to keep her from calling out.

This was how she had been found. Jane Sparrow had gone to investigate why the curtains were closed around this particular bed. Save for exceptional circumstances, it was hospital policy to keep them open to facilitate patient supervision.

"Did you close the curtains, Miss Bennett?" I asked.

Rutherford stiffened.

"*I* closed them, sir," he hastened to say, feeling perhaps that my question implied a criticism of the girl and anxious to demonstrate — better late than never — a sense of responsibility. "The foreign lady pointed at the curtains and made me understand that she wanted them drawn so she could have a better nap."

"What became of her clothes?" I asked the nurses.

"There are drawers in the table by each bed," said Jane Sparrow. "A patient's effects are kept there unless she's one of the ones that might wander off without a proper discharge. The constable warned us that Miss Clarkson might be disoriented on account of a blow to her head, so I put her things in this room. Did you want to see them?"

I nodded. "Please."

While the older nurse was retrieving them from a locked metal cabinet, Miss Bennett turned with a reproving look to Rutherford. "Your warning didn't include the fact that this woman was a dangerous criminal."

"We didn't know," I interjected.

"The police force closes ranks," murmured Miss Bennett, rubbing her wrists.

"Our interest in Lucy Clarkson was as a witness to a crime," I explained, "not a suspect. She'd been hit on the head. We needed the hospital to tell us when she'd be fit to question."

Jane Sparrow rejoined us, with Lucy's rust-coloured rayon dress and a few undergarments folded over one arm and the shoes mended with sticking plaster in the other hand.

"We weren't even able to figure out which languages she speaks," I went on. "Were you?"

"We're nurses," sniffed Miss Bennett, "not linguists."

I was ready to start calling her Daisy just for spite.

"Another patient thought she heard Polish," offered Miss Sparrow. "I wouldn't know."

I looked over the girdle-bra combination Lucy had been wearing when admitted to the hospital. "Do you wear one of these, Miss Bennett?"

Rutherford blushed. "Sergeant, I don't think ..."

"It's a reasonable question," Miss Bennett allowed, all scientific again. "You want to know when you go looking for your runaway witness if she still has the same figure you last saw her with." She fingered the stiff, white undergarment. "I've never found the need of anything this confining. But I suspect Miss Clarkson would have changed her clothes again as soon as she got out of the hospital. On her, mine would have been conspicuously tight. Uncomfortably so too, I'd guess."

"She take any money from you?" I asked. "Enough for a new outfit?"

"Not nearly. There may have been fifty cents in my apron pocket. Snack money is as much as I carry when I'm on duty." She was still fingering Lucy's girdle, I thought absent-mindedly, but then her fingers disappeared into an unexpected opening. "Aha, it seems I made a good trade after all."

From a pocket sewn inside the bottom of the girdle Miss Bennett drew three banknotes; engraved on each was a picture of Benjamin Franklin and the amount $100.

Constable Rutherford whistled his astonishment, a whistle cut short by the sight of Jane Sparrow's finger on her lips.

"That's an awful lot to leave behind," said Miss Bennett. "What was she running away from?"

"We're working to find out." I ran my finger inside the pocket to see if anything else was lurking there. I found nothing except a small key.

Jane Sparrow's thought was as quick as mine. "It looks as if it might fit the suitcase you have there," she said, brown eyes alive with curiosity.

I changed the subject. "Miss Bennett, Lucy Clarkson took your eyeglasses. Could you describe them for us?"

The young nurse laughed. "Look around the hospital, Mr. Policeman. You'll only see one style, regulation style — big round goggles with black metal frames. Utilitarian and uglifying. You can bet the Strangler threw them away as soon as she got to the street. The prescription's not strong, but looking through them would be irritating for anyone with twenty-twenty vision."

I left my name and the HQ phone number before wrapping up the interview. My last question was whether any diagnosis had been made of Lucy Clarkson before her escape. The nurses said no, she'd have been examined when the doctors made their afternoon rounds. I said I was sorry I'd have to take the $300 and carried off Lucy's clothes as well in a brown paper bag supplied by one of the nurses.

I phoned Grace Hospital again from the hospital lobby, only to find that Ned Cruickshank had been and gone. The pathologist told me the man accompanying the acting detective had failed to identify the deceased. When Constable Rutherford asked if we were now going to go looking for Lucy Clarkson, I suggested it was a little late for that, that it had already been too late for hot pursuit by the time he got back from his lunch. Oh, said Rutherford, where then were we going next? I suggested we walk south as far as Bathurst and Queen. From there, he could carry on west back to Parkdale while I boarded a streetcar east to City Hall. The projected parting of the ways spurred the constable to justify himself. He wasn't in the habit of having his equipment stolen, he said. In his years on the force, he'd nabbed more pickpockets than a dog has fleas. It was just, as I myself had said, that the foreign woman wasn't suspected of criminal behaviour. And then her not speaking English meant she had to communicate with him in dumb show, waving her arms about. It had put him off his guard. But he wouldn't be caught twice.

He'd learned his lesson. Maybe so, I said, but I had no work for him at present and he might as well report back to his home station. As for his handcuffs, they were now evidence of a crime and for the time being could not be returned to him.

Once I'd seen Rutherford off on his streetcar, I changed my mind about where to go and took the next car in the same westerly direction. I'd lugged Lucy's suitcase around enough to feel a sense of ownership, and now that I thought I had the means for a discreet look inside I didn't fancy taking that look at my desk with other detectives and possibly the inspector peering over my shoulder. So I retreated to my own bed-sitter apartment and sat with it on the bed.

The key fitted all right. Inside I found a plastic toilet case, a nightie, a negligee, two pair of flesh-coloured stockings, and two pair of loose step-in drawers. Also, a second inexpensive dropped-waist summer dress, this one apple green with red roses printed on it. All cheap but fashionable. Then there was an incongruously dowdy tweed skirt and a white schoolmarmish blouse. Puzzled, I kept digging and came at last to a Commonwealth of Australia passport in the name of Miss Edna Salisbury.

Before opening it, I hung up my jacket, peeled off my sweat-soaked shirt, drew a deep breath, and dared to hope that inside this grey-brown little book I'd find a photograph of the mystery woman.

No such luck. The photo on page three was of someone quite different — a jowly woman with a thick, bumpy nose, and straight, pale hair pulled back behind prominent ears. She was wearing a mannish shirt and tie. That jibed at least with the frumpy blouse in the suitcase, but I wasn't about to start calling its recent possessor Edna just yet.

Particulars were handwritten in black ink. The place and date of birth were given as Melbourne, Victoria, 24th May 1890 — which made Miss Salisbury thirty-six. Her profession appeared as schoolteacher, her domicile Perth. The passport had been issued on 10th August 1925 and was to expire 9th August 1927. The latter pages had been decorated with the rubber stamps of authorities in Western Australia, Ceylon, the United Kingdom, the United States, and — just one day ago — Canada at Niagara Falls.

I took myself for a walk, all of three strides across the room to the bookcase where I kept my Seagram's rye. Prohibition was still in effect in Ontario, and while I didn't expect a raid, I enjoyed pulling out a volume of my second-hand encyclopedia whenever I wanted a drink. The mickey behind *Demijohn to Edward* was just under half full when I took it down, and still had one good plug in it when I tucked it away.

Back on the bed, I went through the suitcase once more, looking for more of those tricky hidden pockets and feeling around for anything sewn inside the lining. I didn't find a thing of either kind, but this time I opened the toilet case.

I was expecting a toothbrush, a hair brush, a tube of lipstick, and maybe some face powder. All present and accounted for, but there was stage makeup as well — putty and greasepaint — and hair dye.

Chapter 6

WARSAW — AN EVENING IN early August under an uncertain sky. Lucy had a train to catch, but the station she'd known from her student days had been demolished five years earlier, and construction had yet to start on the replacement. Her soon to be ex-lover Jan Tomczak took her and her suitcase to the temporary station on Chmielna Street. The suitcase and most of the clothes it contained (with sleeves shortened and hemlines raised) were castoffs of Wanda's. Lucy's friend had also given her a home-baked poppyseed cake for the journey. They had said their goodbyes early to avoid emotional platform scenes.

When the boat train to the new Polish port of Gdynia started to board, Jan didn't waste their last moments together on hollow endearments. Instead, he wanted to give her advice. He impressed upon Lucy that the British were big on proper channels of communication. Ultimately, she'd want to get her information into the hands of the Secret Intelligence Service, but as the United Kingdom never admitted to spying on other states she couldn't approach MI6 directly. Her best route would be through Scotland Yard's eminently respectable Special Branch. Even though their mandate was confined to counter-intelligence and counterterrorism, they would have access to the shadowy spymasters that briefed Whitehall.

The train trip and sea voyage passed without incident. In London, a modest daily donation secured her one of twenty small guest rooms in the house of the Sisters of Saint Hedwig. During her first days in the city, she had some dental work done to repair the damage Trigorin had caused. At the same time, remembering the threatening car in Warsaw, she cast about for a means of speedy escape. She pored over ship and railway schedules. The hostel's practice of collecting passports of foreign guests at check-in and retaining them for the full duration of their stay gave her an idea for disguise. She studied the other women with a view to choosing which she might, with a little stage makeup, impersonate. Her first choice had to be ruled out when it transpired that the woman, a Czechoslovak, was leaving in three days. The runner-up, an Australian, had an educational conference to attend plus visits to pay to a number of grammar schools in the London area, all of which would take her at least two and a half weeks. The trouble was that Edna was appreciably shorter than Lucy. Lucy could only hope that in the next day or so, as residents came and went, a better fit would show up.

At the same time, she got on with her mission, presenting her true identity documents at New Scotland Yard on the Victoria Embankment. She had taken the risk of travelling to Britain under her own name, had even ventured into Warsaw's New Town to obtain a copy of her certificate of baptism from St. Kazimierz Church. The desk bobbies kept her waiting while they made telephone calls. She was prepared to be suspected of being a crank, but was eventually given an appointment for the next day, August 18. Two men interviewed her, Messrs. North and Green. North, the younger, was well-tailored and well-educated, blond, confident, polite. The older one — by twelve or fifteen years — had a worried look; he was rumpled, corpulent, balding, and spectacled.

Green peered at Lucy through his thick lenses and got her to tell her story. North asked follow-up questions. Both men looked at her photographic prints. Then Green asked if Lucy could remain in London for a few weeks. She said she could if she were given a cover identity and documents permitting her to work. Green said he'd look into it. He didn't offer government money. She wasn't looking for it: being believed at the highest level would be payment enough. North asked her about the women's hostel and told her to inform them of any change of address. And she might as well hand over the negatives from which the document prints were made.

Lucy demurred. In that case, North didn't see that they could extract full value from her discovery. The prints she had shown them were up to the standard of a commercial photo shop, but His Majesty's Government had more sophisticated equipment that stood an excellent chance of making any blurred print legible. Lucy said she'd think this over. Green hastened to say that would be satisfactory. Nothing moved at breakneck speed in the civil service, he noted. They would doubtless be dealing with this business for weeks to come, if not months. Relieved and discouraged at once, Lucy asked if the two men didn't think her discovery of this breach of the Versailles Treaty significant. Of course, North promptly replied. Germany's perfidy was what men of his generation had been suspecting for years, and it was jolly good to get hold of some proof. Green smiled regretfully and said that security considerations prevented them from telling her how her contribution confirmed, extended, or contradicted what Britain already knew. But they appreciated the long and dangerous journey she had undertaken to bring these photos to them. They would be in touch.

Lucy had been hoping that within days if not hours of her revelations she would be reading in the *Times* of parliamentarians denouncing the Russo-German military pact. It now seemed that she was in for a long and dreary wait. She never had waited well: patience was the one espionage asset she knew she lacked. She had some sense of London from her time here five years earlier, but naturally could not get in touch with any of her previous contacts, had indeed to avoid any places she might run into members of the CPGB.

Someone she did run into, two days after meeting Green and North at the Yard, was the latter, at the self-serve restaurant of a Lyons Corner House. North expressed pleasure at the chance encounter. He asked her to call him Harry and suggested they share a table. He said there was a sit-down dining room upstairs where they could have wine if she'd prefer. She replied that tea was fine.

They drank a lot of tea. Harry North said he was from the Midlands and had only been in town a couple of years himself. He sounded more tentative and timid than during working hours, though he did his bit to keep conversation going. He gathered Lucy hadn't had much playtime recently. Well, London was the place to catch up. Did she like the theatre? *No, No, Nanette* was still on at the Palace. Perhaps she preferred the cinema. Did she dance? Play any games? Lucy merrily claimed to be the Soviet women's golf champion, as well as to play ice hockey, polo, and football. He laughed and asked her about water polo. Did she swim? Yes. Seriously? She liked to swim, she told him, sincerely if not seriously. She was enjoying herself too much to be serious. He asked if he could take her to Hampstead Ponds on the weekend.

She said she had no bathing suit. "On the continent we swim naked. Would that be all right?"

Harry's face turned pink. "Steady on. We're just getting used to mixed sex bathing here. Not to worry. The city Parks Department can likely rent us a costume for you. Just a light wool covering neck to knees — probably in navy or black."

"Every woman's dream."

They drained their teacups for the last time, and he walked her back to the Sisters of Saint Hedwig in time for her curfew.

Only when they were out on the street did Harry North refer to the photographs. He said that at their last meeting he hadn't wanted to scare her, but that London could be a dangerous place. The negatives would really be safer with him. Did she have them with her? No? In her room then? Harry would wait on the pavement while she got them. She said they weren't in her room either, adding that she understood his fear but that she had hidden them well. He looked into her eyes with a look that started in kindly concern and ended in admiration. He said he'd pick her up the next afternoon at three.

Lucy could not make up her mind about Harry. For the first hour after she went to bed, she didn't feel she had a mind, so absorbed was she by fantasies of the elegant blond Englishman. When these at last started to bore her, she turned on the light and washed her face. Time to see where she stood. She wanted to believe she was making a useful ally of the secret service agent. But his insistence on taking her negatives set off alarm bells. And she was quite sure that thoughts of her in his arms had not deprived him of any sleep this night. More alarm bells: she had trained to be the swallow, not the swallowed.

Saturday morning, Lucy spent the last of Jan Tomczak's money on a bathing costume — just in case the ones for rent were as hideous as they sounded.

The garment she bought was lime green with thin straps that left her shoulders bare; it stopped six inches above the knee. She had just enough pennies left over for a red rubber cap.

Harry's cab arrived punctually at three. He tried to light a cigarette for her twice on the drive up to Hampstead Heath and dropped the match each time. The third time, Lucy held his hand steady. She asked if he wanted to peek at what was in her Marks and Spencer shopping bag. He said he'd rather wait and see it on her. Lucy had never met a man nervousness became so well.

At the ponds, Lucy and Harry were each assigned a cubicle in which to change and leave their street clothes. When she'd changed, Lucy left the key to the cubicle with the women's attendant and received a token bearing the same number as the key. She attached the token as instructed to the shoulder strap of her bathing costume and when she met Harry out on the terrace noticed he had done the same. When Harry saw her green swimsuit, he called it "abso-bally-lutely smashing," and it really sounded to Lucy as if he meant it as high praise.

One end of the mixed bathing pond, the highest of the three in Hampstead Heath, was full of families — mothers and fathers, brothers and sisters — enjoying the chance to swim together, but there was lots of open water further from shore. Despite the warmth of the summer day, the water was cold. Lucy didn't mind, except that she was afraid her goosebumps made her arms ugly. She distracted Harry by challenging him to a race, then smelled a rat when she won. In the rematch, she sternly insisted he go flat out. When she finally caught up to him at the finish line, he was wearing a sheepish grin. She scooped water in his face and told him she liked him all the better for not trying to make it close. They splashed about until their lips turned blue and Harry suggested they get dressed and have some tea.

When she exchanged her token for her cubicle key, the motherly attendant told her she could see from Lucy's face that she'd had a good bathe. Lucy realized that all the time she'd been in the pond she hadn't had a single thought of German warplanes — and still she couldn't wipe the smile off her face. She unlocked her cubicle. When she was inside with the door closed, light came through openings front and back just below the ceiling. She peeled off her suit and wrung it out well so it wouldn't soak through her paper shopping bag. She took care not to dribble water into her shoes. That's when she noticed there was something different about them. They were patent leather Mary Janes she had picked up in Warsaw and cleaned up this morning with a little spit and toilet paper. She'd carelessly left one upright and one on its side when she'd changed earlier, and that's the way she found them. But the insole in the upright one was now wrinkled. She squatted down and ran two fingers over the wrinkles. That insole was loose. She stuck her fingers into the other shoe and found its insole loose too. Both had been securely glued down at noon. She shivered now not just from the cold water. Just minutes ago, while she'd been frolicking with

Harry, her effects had been searched for the thirty-five millimetre negatives. An expert job betrayed by a lack of glue.

When she met Harry, Lucy said she had a headache and was sorry she could not go for tea. In the taxi, Harry looked uncomfortable. Lucy wondered whether he suspected she'd found out about the search. Or was he just trying to appear sympathetic to her pain?

It was hard to believe he was innocent in the affair. The swim had been a dream opportunity to have her clothes picked over. She supposed the British secret service couldn't let a foreign woman — especially one that spoke English so badly — hold out on them. They had tried first the gentlest path to their goal. They could still lock her up until she gave them the negatives. It would be done with all possible civility, no need to kill her. A darker prospect, however, had seized Lucy's imagination. Suppose Harry were a closet Communist playing a double game, ostensibly working for Great Britain while owing his true allegiance to Soviet Russia. Then her life wouldn't be worth two kopecks. Her safest course was to assume the worst and get far away from Harry North.

He made comments on the areas of London they were passing through on the way back to her hostel in the Victoria Station neighbourhood. When she didn't respond, he asked if his chatter helped distract her, as he intended, or just made things worse. She told him to talk if he liked — it didn't bother her — only he must not mind if she wasn't able to answer. Thinking the couple would enjoy a view of the river this summer evening, the driver departed from the most direct route to take them down the Embankment. Passing New Scotland Yard gave Lucy the idea of asking Harry whether Mr. Green had managed to secure her new visa and work permit. When he answered not, Lucy scarcely had to murmur that that put her in a difficult position. With becoming reticence, Harry produced his billfold and asked her if as a special favour to him Lucy would accept a modest loan. He fanned out a few banknotes so that she could make the loan as modest as she chose. As if blinded by the pounding in her head, Lucy clutched them all. She smiled bravely at him then, told him he was sweet. As they parted at her front door, he kissed her cheek and expressed sorrow that their afternoon had ended so unfortunately. He promised to be in touch.

In her room, Lucy found what she expected: traces of an expert but not undetectable search. She now wasn't sure whether the job had been botched or whether she'd been meant to be intimidated by the knowledge that OGPU had her in their sights. If it was indeed OGPU and not MI6, she knew what the next step must be: capture and interrogation. In the basement of the Lubianka, a prisoner could be broken down so gradually that a warder could look himself in the mirror at night and not see a torturer. But in the field an agent was always rushed and under-equipped. You might have to improvise with a blade under the fingernail, a cigarette lighter under the ear. Lucy didn't know what all: that hadn't been her department. But she had known not to ask. She also knew enough of how OGPU worked abroad to believe she would not be dragged from her room. They would wait till she went out, until she was walking alone on the street. Even a busy street. A car would stop just long enough for her to be pushed into the back and would speed away before bystanders had time to comprehend, let alone intervene.

That Saturday evening, Lucy did not leave her room. She went without supper. After the curfew, the office by the front door was not staffed. To be extra certain that all the inmates of the house were in their beds, Lucy waited until one a.m. Then she crept downstairs. The office door lock had not been changed in fifty years and yielded readily to someone with Lucy's training. The Sisters of Saint Hedwig made no secret of which desk drawer held residents' passports.

Lucy removed Edna Salisbury's, no taller candidate for impersonation having shown up. Perhaps she could avoid comment on her longer legs by using a wheelchair at checkpoints. While her accented and fractured English sorted strangely with her new alias, she was prepared to say that her Australian father had died shortly after her birth in Melbourne and that her Polish mother had taken her back to Cracow, where she'd lived until age twenty. At that point, she'd returned to Australia as a teacher of European languages.

Lucy relocked the office on her way out and returned to her room.

OGPU might have a car stationed outside the Sisters' front door on Belgrave Road, particularly if they believed Lucy knew her belongings had been inspected. But her main reason for not leaving immediately was that she wanted there to be nothing suspicious about her departure. Both front and rear doors to the hostel were bolted from the inside at night. If in the morning either bolt were found drawn, an investigation was liable to ensue, and the theft of Edna's passport might be discovered.

Lucy had to get out of England. She would try the United States: they were the great power now. Americans had spent cash and blood on the Allied victory. The last thing they'd want would be a remilitarized Germany. Neither would such staunch capitalists want the Soviet Union deploying modern warplanes to attack and gobble up its neighbours.

At one twenty, Lucy sat down on her bed and began studying how her new acquisition might help her reach Washington. Finding that two strokes of a pen would increase the bearer's height from five foot one to five foot four made her almost giddy with excitement. Good luck meant nothing to her beyond itself; she took it as no sign of divine favour. But fortune hadn't smiled on her mission in either Warsaw or London. So when luck came, even in small parcels, it deserved its moment of celebration.

Continuing her study, Lucy found still more to cheer about. Edna's passport was endorsed for the entire British Empire, excluding only Palestine, Mesopotamia, and Egypt. So she could enter Canada. From there, the U.S. border shouldn't prove much of an obstacle. If she could get out of Russia, she could get into America. But wait — she saw that, in the endorsement section on page four, a line had been left blank. Just the opening for an OGPU-trained forger. Immediately below *British Empire*, she could write *United States* in the same bureaucratic hand and spare herself the inconvenience of smuggling herself in. Sleeping that night was like eating when you feel full. Lucy did it only by an effort of will and because the next day would be a long one.

She checked out at seven thirty a.m., leaving on foot in the midst of a group of residents attending the eight o'clock mass at Westminster Cathedral. Lucy was pretty sure no abduction would be risked so long as she was in the middle of this crowd. Along the way, she tried to spot a car rolling suspiciously slowly or a man stalking the cluster of women with something besides lechery on his mind. She saw nothing of the kind, although it didn't escape her that her tail might be one of the cluster, the same woman perhaps that had searched her room.

During Mass, Lucy sat where she could see all her hostel-mates, taking leave of them after the Dismissal and Recessional. Then, to be on the safe side, she executed a number of feints. She jumped on omnibuses only to jump off as soon as she could switch to one going the opposite way. She boarded a train with a ticket to Dover, but got off at Maidstone. Her options were limited by Sunday schedules; nevertheless, by a combination of rail, bus, and hitchhiking, she made it to Southampton before midnight with the conviction that she had not been followed.

The ship on which Lucy booked passage to New York didn't leave until early afternoon, which gave her time to shop for dowdy clothes, makeup, pen, and ink and to use her purchases to redecorate herself and the stolen passport to make them better agree. She lightened her suitcase by discarding all items not fitting her Edna Salisbury identity. She also practised Edna's signature. It helped her that it was so copybook conventional and lacking individual character. A signature meant to be written slowly and carefully — on a blackboard, perhaps, to introduce Miss Salisbury to her pupils on the first day of school. If called upon to use it in front of other people, Lucy would have to look at home with the signature, but would never have to dash it off.

During the nine-day crossing on the USS *Luxuria*, Lucy maintained this identity, without passing up the pleasures of the dinner table or the gaming table. She had a good head and good nerves for cards, which her schoolmarmish appearance belied. A day out of Southampton, she had recouped the cost of her first-class passage with pennies to spare, then made a killing on the last night before docking in New York. The last opportunity for legal drinking and its attendant frenzy took her by surprise. Next day they would be crossing the three-mile limit into U.S. territorial waters, where the Volstead Act prohibited the recreational consumption of alcohol. Any beer, wine, or spirits would be placed under seal until the ship crossed the line again heading east. Such a prospect must have seemed too drab for some passengers, for rumours persisted that all the ship's liquid treasure would be dumped over the side, and what a waste that would be! Better to drink hearty and leave nothing for the fishes. Lucy had not seen the bacchanal coming; it amazed her. All the same, she limited herself to three brandies for the evening and profited from the reckless play of her pie-eyed fellow passengers.

The risks of poker were nothing to her compared to the higher-stakes risk of arriving in New York with a stolen passport. The real Edna, if she'd kept to her intended timetable, wouldn't yet have finished her school visits. The theft wouldn't be discovered for another ten days. That was the course of events Lucy had gambled on. It was quite possible, however, that Harry North had come to the hostel asking after Lucy and her headache the day following their Hampstead Pond swim. Suspicious at her sudden departure, he'd have instigated a police investigation. If competently done, that investigation would have revealed that Edna's passport was gone. Then the checking of ships' passenger lists would have begun, starting with ships bound for British Empire ports. Finding that no one identifying herself as Edna Salisbury had gone aboard, would they assume that Lucy and the passport were still in the United Kingdom? Or suspect that the document had been tampered with and see where that hypothesis might lead?

Chapter 7

I'D NEVER SEEN ANYTHING like this case. As a rule, a scarf tied over a holdup man's face was the most sophisticated disguise a Toronto detective ever had to deal with. The big, wide, devious world — Europe and now Australia — seemed to be crowding in on our bustling but parochial town. After treating myself to a cool shower and a clean shirt, I packed clothes, passport, theatrical makeup, and all back into Lucy's suitcase and took it and myself downtown, with a stop on the way at the lab of the University of Toronto chemistry professor.

Police headquarters overfilled the wing of City Hall into which it had been poured, spilling out by a couple of desks into the wide corridor. You'd think the brass would be grateful to me for doing my bit to relieve congestion, including staying away as much as possible. Inspector Sanderson was sore all the same. For some reason, he thought me overdue, and he told me he was docking me two days' pay. The threat had become such an old wheeze with him that a month and a half earlier — back in the sleepy middle of July — he'd actually followed through and done it. He loved to save the department's money. He even believed I'd thank him for punishing my absences monetarily rather than by putting a black mark in my file. I was spending nearly what I earned, so I was less than fulsome in my thanks. Keeping out of lunchrooms and coffee shops during that lean time, not to mention withholding business from the butcher and the rum-runner, had been a bore, particularly as I'd no big investigation then. Still, I was an old hand at doing without, and the sentence would seem shorter this time so long as I was able to make progress on the Beaconsfield case.

In the exams you take to become an inspector of detectives, I'll bet Sanderson got a first-class grade in scowling. His natural advantages were a high, pious forehead, fenced off from ice blue eyes by his single, thick eyebrow — which he may have improved on nature by dyeing black. His preacherly voice was carrying, so to save him embarrassment I shut his office door whenever he dressed me down.

Today I got a five-minute scolding. With that out of the way, he started fiddling with his pipe and looked almost human. I opened the door again. Sanderson's fumigation-strength tobacco always made me cough. Still, once he lit up I knew he was ready to listen.

Ready to a point.

"Now don't start by cluttering my brain with all the facts and testimony you've collected, Paul. Lead off with your theory of this bomb blast or whatever it was. Make sense of it if you can."

I set aside the notes I'd scribbled on the streetcar. "It looks to me like an accident," I said, "though hardly an innocent one. The dead bird — we don't know his name — wasn't innocently in that hotel. I haven't eye-balled every one of the registered guests, but either he wasn't one of them or he has one of the clerks lying for him. It's my belief that someone in the hotel, guest or clerk, let him in."

"How would a guest do that?" asked Sanderson.

"By lowering the fire escape. Now what was this John Doe doing in the hotel? And what was he doing with a bomb? We can rule out suicide: he was hold-ing the bomb away from his body when it went off. It looked like he was about to throw it. The bomb must have been defective in some way — or, even more likely if it was a grenade, the thrower lost track of the number of seconds he had left before detonation. From an analysis of residue on the deceased's shirt, Professor Linacre has concluded that the explosive agent was the standard mixture of TNT and barium nitrate used in British 'Mills bomb' hand grenades since early in the war. The position of the body suggested Doe was about to launch his projectile through the transom window of Room 29, occupied at the time by a woman registered under the name Lucy Clarkson. The blast knocked the door off its hinges so that it fell on and stunned Miss Clarkson. I had her sent to the Toronto Western Hospital — where she assaulted a nurse and left before she could be seen by a doctor."

"Oh? And where was this constable you sent with her to the Western?"

"Dipping his moustaches in a bowl of soup. Strictly AWOL."

The inspector had nothing to say to that.

"My theory," I went on, "is that Doe died in the course of an attempt on Miss Clarkson's life and that she is afraid of either police scrutiny or a renewed attempt, or both."

"So who is Lucy Clarkson," mused Sanderson, "and what makes her worth killing?"

"Dunno, sir." I refrained from pointing out that we'd have had a better chance of knowing if I'd been the one to watch over her at the Western. "It *looks* like she arrived from the United States yesterday using the passport of an Australian woman named Edna Salisbury. The passport appears to have been issued for both the British Empire and the United States, but Professor Linacre has concluded that the U.S. endorsement was added in different ink and in a different hand. Linacre further finds that the height given for Miss Salisbury has been altered from 5 feet 1 inch to 5 feet 4 inches by the addition of two pen strokes, again in that same second black ink."

"Is Lucy Clarkson 5 foot 4?"

"If she slouches," I said. "I suspect Clarkson is another alias, inspired by the name of a village she would have passed through on the way here from Niagara Falls. She is European in appearance and may speak one or more Slavic languages. No one I've spoken to yet has heard a word of English from her.

She was carrying three hundred dollars in American currency, which she left behind when she fled the hospital. If the money was stolen, the grenade might have been intended as a punishment for the theft. The fact that John Doe was wearing a Macy's department store jacket raises the possibility that he followed her here from New York."

A ringing phone on Sanderson's desk put an end to his cross-examination. He asked the caller to hang on and, with his hand over the mouthpiece, whispered to me my marching orders.

"See if the mob is involved, Paul — an American gang with ties to criminal organizations in Canada. That would account for the local accomplice. But not a word to the press. This is the *Examiner* on the line now. Leave the interviews to me."

I said I'd be glad to.

"And for the rest, just follow your nose and let me know where it leads. You might try to find the foreign woman — just a suggestion. You're as good a detective as I have. I don't need to tell you your business."

Before I could test whether the compliment was worth bonus pay, the inspector was purring into the phone and waving me out of his smoke-clouded office.

And that was that. The grenade explosion was reported in the Saturday edition of the major dailies — along with the renewal of negotiations to end the British coal strike and the *Examiner* management's promise to continue publication of the paper in the event of a walkout by their typesetters. Throughout the city, most work was suspended for the Labour

Day holiday weekend. While the police didn't close up shop, the Beaconsfield investigation seemed for the next two days to mark time. The veteran Detective Sergeant Knight, Acting Detective Ned Cruickshank, a couple of constables (not including the disgraced Rutherford), and I pursued various inquiries, but got little or less to show for them.

Knight, the dean of the detective department, had had experience with the Black Hand extortion racket, so we worked it out that he'd start on the mobster angle. He soon discovered how stale his list of contacts had become. His next inspiration was to investigate the two men associated with the Beaconsfield who bore Italian names. Owner Joe Ferraro turned out to have been a Torontonian for over thirty years and had no known criminal associations. Nor could any link be established between him and either the bomber or Lucy Clarkson. Hotel guest Leo Di Giovanni provided a list of his Toronto contacts, mostly merchants along College Street west of Bathurst; all vouched for him as a sales representative of Taste of the Homeland Italian Foods. He was forthcoming also about the other North American towns where he peddled his oils and cheeses. Telegrams were sent to the respective police departments; none reported back anything against him. The Italian identity papers he showed Knight gave Florence as his place of birth and residence. Unlike the other guests, Di Giovanni admitted to having seen the woman from Room 29. He'd tried to ask her to have dinner with him Thursday night, but had given up when the two appeared to have no language in common.

Ned and the boys in uniform were meanwhile busying themselves with background checks on the other hotel guests. They reported that Dan Ewart, son of a Glace Bay miner, had served as a corporal with the Princess Louise Fusiliers during the war and through most of the years since had set type for the Halifax papers *Morning Herald, Chronicle*, and *Evening Mail*. He had got himself in minor trouble down east distributing left-wing literature. Floyd Peters, the young telegraphist, turned out to be active in the Canadian Brotherhood of Railway Employees. He was also helping promote the formation of a super-union, but had no links to any political party. Ernest Pollard, on the other hand, the registered occupant of Room 25 the morning of the explosion, had once run (unsuccessfully) for the provincial legislature under the banner of the progressive, pro-temperance United Farmers of Ontario. Pollard had returned safely to his orchard near Brighton and therefore could not be John Doe.

I didn't see that any of this got us very far.

Try to find the foreign woman. I tried, Inspector, and how! Working outwards from the Toronto Western Hospital, I spent most of Saturday visiting businesses within a five-block radius. In addition, I must have interviewed every streetcar conductor on the Bathurst and Dundas lines. I described Lucy/Edna every which way I could think of. I made allowance for the fact that I'd seen her only as a recovering bomb victim and surely not at her best — in appearance, vim, or mental capacity. My general impression was of a full-figured, sturdily built individual, close in age to myself, with somewhat exotic features. I gave details of hair and eye colour, skin texture, approximate height and weight. No one had noticed her. It was as if one of those stunt flyers had swooped down in a biplane and hoisted her into the sky.

Speaking of flying, I had an unexpected conversation on the subject with the Beaconsfield night clerk. A complete contrast to day man Frank Gabor, Alex Horvath was clean-shaven and alert. It was after nine when I dropped in Saturday night, fully dark but still so hot and muggy that the lobby door had been propped open. With long, quick fingers, Horvath was dealing himself a neatly squared patience layout without ever taking his eyes off the entrance. His kisser had enough of the Valentino look that you wouldn't let your girl anywhere near him. I put his age at about thirty, which meant that — barring some disqualifying health problem — he'd likely fought in the war. He gave me a silent but encouraging nod when I mentioned my name and business.

"What language did Lucy Clarkson use when she registered?" I hadn't intended this to be my first question, but my eye had caught the *Mann spricht Deutsch* sign on the desk, a sign I hadn't seen there during the day shift.

Horvath's right hand tapped the sign on the way to placing a red jack on a black queen.

"Did it sound as if German was her first language?"

Horvath placed a second ace at the top of his layout. I was wondering if I was going to get a word out of him. Then he seemed to finish his appraisal of me and decided to open up.

"Her first language? Not really, but then I perhaps would not know. It's not mine either. I learned the rudiments in Budapest, and added a bit of polish in the Austro-Hungarian Air Force."

"In Russia?"

"The Italian Front. There were British troops there too." He looked me up and down. "Perhaps eight or nine years ago you and I were trying to kill each other."

"I was crawling around trenches in Flanders," I said, "safely out of your way. But there were Canadian flyers there, some pretty well-known ones at that. Would you ever have tangled with William Barker?"

Horvath laughed at the suggestion. "You think I'd be alive to talk about it?"

"Or Christopher Whitehead?" I asked, remembering a paragraph on Kip's postings in Friday's newspaper article.

The clerk demolished his layout, which was plainly doomed, and slowly put the pack of cards aside.

"Whitehead, yes."

I waited to see if he'd say more. And he did, a lot more.

"It was February 1918 — cold already at ground level, and we were always flying at altitude to avoid ploughing into the Alps. The higher you went, the lower the temperature. Cockpits weren't heated, forget enclosed, so every bit of clothing was needed. Even with all your kit in place, frostbite was routine."

I saw I was in for a full-blown soldier's tale — one rehearsed over long, empty nights at the hotel desk. But the case wasn't dragging me in any other direction. I was happy to let Horvath talk, although I did try to move things along a little.

"Okay," I said, "It was cold. What then?"

"Then, one morning, I was unlucky enough to be flying without gloves. I'd loaned mine to some-one who'd lost his in a *taverna* and then got himself shot down wearing mine — a long story. But it's the day I'm wearing socks on my hands and can hardly feel the controls that I find myself in the sights of the twin Vickers of a Sopwith Camel. I do this and this." Horvath's right hand sketched in the air the evasive dodging and diving of his plane.

"Were you able to return fire?" I asked.

"A few bursts, but with no feeling in my fingers I could hit nothing. My hands were like bears' paws." Horvath wasn't looking at me anymore but through me to that winter morning in northern Italy. "The mountain air was so clear and we danced around each other so tightly that I could see the drops of castor oil that had splashed back from his engine onto the lenses of his goggles. Yeah, the devil of it was that his Camel could turn more tightly than my Albatros. Suddenly my engine stopped. I was going down. Now, I thought, I'm his on a plate. He followed me down, and still he didn't fire."

Horvath left a pause for the wonder of that restraint to sink in, but I was curious and nudged him on. "You made a deadstick landing."

"Messing up a nice snowy field. On impact, my machine flipped, wheels and the propeller broken off. I knew I had landed on our side of the Piave River, but a long walk from our nearest outpost. I crawled out from under the wreckage." He mimed the action, looking warily up through the lobby ceiling for his attacker at the same time. "That's when the Camel came swooping down for one more pass. Just over my head, the pilot leaned out of his cockpit. And dropped his big leather flying gloves in the snow beside me."

"Did you know who it was?"

"Not then. But you can bet I memorized the number on the side of his plane as he lifted its nose and headed west. I hoped he made it home to breakfast before his hands froze. When I rejoined my squadron, old-timers told me who flies that plane. Sure enough I found the initials C.W. stitched into the cuffs."

How like Kip, I thought with a smile. In Horvath's place, I'd have wanted to meet him. "So after the war," I said, "you came to this country to return the gloves?"

"Return nothing! Every time Whitehead sets a new flying record, the value of these gloves goes up. When his fame reaches maximum altitude, I'll sell and retire. My reason for coming to Canada? It's more like *Mrs.* Whitehead's."

"Politics?"

"There's an article about her in *Maclean's*." Horvath was gesturing towards the lobby's tableful of old magazines. "Look for yourself!"

I flipped through the well-thumbed pages till I came to a recent photo of a broadly smiling Bea

Whitehead — holding her arms out like wings, as if she could fly without the plane she stood in front of. She wore an elegant sportswoman's tailored shirt and trousers, but no helmet. I guessed the point was to show off her abundance of blond hair freshly done up in Marcel waves. It hadn't escaped my notice that makers of beauty products advertised in the magazine.

My own memory flashed up a similarly playful image of Bea, the one time I'd seen her. That would have been early summer, 1925. The Whiteheads were visiting Miles Sutton, a Toronto financier Kip hoped to enlist as a sponsor of his Calgary flight. The couple had driven down from Ottawa in their Hispano-Suiza, which had on the night of their arrival daringly been nicked from their host's new Bayview Avenue estate. (The long, winding driveway was still nothing but mud, and they'd had to park near the gates.) Through contacts at an illegal drinking hole I frequented, I tracked the car to a garage in the harbour area, but repainted and with different plates: I needed Kip to confirm the heap was his. When I went to pick him up at the Sutton place, I found him on the lawn trying to teach his wife to play tennis. She was short, softly round, and bursting with style. Like the tournament winners, she wore a bandeau down around her forehead to keep the hair out of her eyes — except that Bea's headband was evening wear, slender and all black sequins. She dithered teasingly over which hand should hold the racquet, and from what I could see, she really could hit the ball forcefully enough and equally accurately with either. The dilemma set her giggling — irrepressibly, and yet as musically as if she'd been the heroine of an operetta. Kip was making no progress, but was enjoying her high spirits too much to care.

I was pleased to find neither one of them suicidal over the loss of more than ten thousand dollars worth of automobile. Still, when I told him my errand, Kip was appreciative, and even more so upon identifying the car I'd run down. Just how often do you hear of the nicest guys pairing with the most amusing girls? I was more than ready to read something about how the Whiteheads got together.

The *Maclean's* article that wrapped around the aviatrix photo told how Bea had met Kip in Treviso, near his aerodrome, and how from the start it had been more than the standard casual contact between local girl and foreign flyer. The two were separated when he was redeployed to the Western Front in the fall of 1918 and then to Hendon air base in England after the war. But they kept writing letters.

Some books and periodicals soft-pedalled what had been happening in Italy. Not this magazine. It let Bea remind its readers that back in her country ex-soldiers and assorted louts had been dressing up in black and tormenting folks in the name of their new philosophy of Fascism. Bea's father's print shop was vandalized one night because he printed a newspaper the blackshirts didn't like. When Fascist bigwig Mussolini became prime minister, Bea's classroom references to blackshirt tactics got her sacked from the school where she'd been teaching. Worse was to come. Left jobless, Bea went to work in her father's shop. Something printed there again attracted the attention of the thugs, during working hours this time. As Bea told it, they beat her father to death with cudgels, then set fire to the place, destroying both the business and the attached apartment. Without livelihood, home, or family, Bea ran away to Switzerland. When she was able to write to Kip, he insisted she join him in London, where he married her in the fall of 1923. He brought her back to Canada the following year. In Ottawa, she'd learned to fly in order to share Kip's passion. And, Bea had told *Maclean's*, to show that the Fascists hadn't doused her daring spirit.

Bea a teacher? It was hard for someone who'd been taught as I had by tired, middle-aged men and women of unquestioning minds to imagine anyone so young and defiant in front of a class. Glancing again at the glamour photo of a soft, fun-loving girl with extended arms, I tried to see the inner steel she would have needed. Courage in the face of danger — that was something she and Kip shared. It must have been a large part of what drew them together.

"Politics," Horvath said when I'd tossed the magazine back on the pile. "But for higher stakes than they put on the table in Ottawa. In my country, paramilitary bands sprang up after the war to break heads and establish a Fascist-style regime."

"What are the odds?"

"I didn't wait to see. The government tolerates them, even negotiates with them. They're the mirror image of Mussolini's gang — full of hate and hungry for another war. No more of that for me, thanks.

Quietly I began to plan my exit from Hungary. For Beatrice Sarto, departure was a little more urgent. She was a marked woman in Italy."

I asked the night clerk if he were a Communist or had ever talked about Communism to a hotel guest named Dan Ewart. He said no to both questions and had nothing else to contribute to the investigation, so I went upstairs to speak to Ewart myself.

He came to his hotel room door in pyjamas, though his bed was still made. Likely he just wanted to keep cool and wasn't expecting visitors. He was tall, but not imposing. Stooped and tentative, rather. Black hair slicked back over either ear left his head bald in the centre. A notebook stood open on the dresser with a pen and a bottle of ink beside it. Judging by the spidery script, I thought that bottle would last him a good long time.

He claimed to be an out-of-work typesetter from Halifax. His story squared with what Ned Cruickshank had already gathered. By now I'd read the pamphlet Ewart had been distributing. It had nothing in it about armed revolution in this country or the establishment here of a dictatorship of the proletariat. All the same, I reminded him that the Communist Party of Canada had for the last seven years been an illegal organization, and that even if under normal circumstances a hard-working police detective had better things to do than throw him in jail for handing out bum-fodder, when found in the vicinity of exploding bombs he should prepare to be suspected. He took off the reading glasses over which he had been peering at me and pointed out that he had left the hotel for the day before the explosion. I asked if he had ever been on the hotel fire escape. His meek features expressed as much surprise and denial as I thought they were capable of. I showed him a photo of John Doe, whom he claimed never to have seen in his life.

The talk at the front desk about Fascism reminded me of Bartholomew Rogers's bedside reading, so I made a call on him next. Rogers, a beefy man of medium height, left no doubt that I was intruding. He came to the door with a cigarette dangling from his lip and his book in his hand, a thick finger marking his place. By his abrupt account, the author's view was anti-Mussolini rather than pro. I confirmed this bias on the basis of my own inspection, which his impatience tended to make more thorough rather than less. I then ran through my questions about John Doe and Lucy Clarkson. Rogers claimed never to have seen or heard about either one. When asked if he'd let anyone into the hotel from the fire escape Friday morning, he raised his voice in indignant denial.

One floor up, I found Hasty MacDermid, perched on the edge of his bed, whistling "Tea for Two" and sponging soot stains from his grey suit. His room smelled like a dry cleaning shop.

I asked him if at any time during his stay he'd opened the hall window outside his door, the window onto the fire escape.

"Never occurred to me. What's that got to do with the price of eggs?"

I hadn't decided how far I wanted to take Hasty into my confidence. For one thing, I hadn't seen him since we'd got home from Europe in May 1919. For another, our acquaintance overseas had been comradely rather than close. Could I swear he was incapable of involvement in a crime? Honestly, no. I'd known him as a brave platoon commander, well-liked by his men, and I'd have written any complimentary nonsense about him for a job reference. Among officers, his stubborn optimism made him the butt of jokes, which he always seemed to take in good part. I couldn't see Lieutenant Hastings MacDermid involved in any sort of gangland vendetta. But both army tradition and our own inclination had banned politics from mess conversation, and it was too soon for me to exclude international intrigue from this latest case of mine.

"We think the bomber — John Doe to his Toronto friends — wasn't staying here, but was let into the hotel by someone that was."

"For the purpose of killing the grey-eyed goddess with the thighs of a channel-swimmer."

"I never said —"

"She sounds charming," Hasty broke in. "I bet you fell in love at first sight."

"My first sight was her feet sticking out from under her hotel room door. They were all right as feet go, but I could have been giving my heart to a corpse."

"Who'd want her dead?"

"A swimming rival for all I know."

"Why not ask the lady?"

"That's a thought. Say, do you think it's healthy to be breathing all that cleaning fluid?"

"It's only carbon tetrachloride, the same stuff that's in the fire extinguisher I use to put out the burning car engine. They give me this shiny new roadster to set on fire several times each day. You really have to see it."

"Sure," I said. Something gold-coloured on the lapel of the jacket in Hasty's hands caught my eye. "What's that pin?"

He unfastened it from the fabric and showed it to me up close. It was shaped like a bundle of sticks with an axe sticking out of them.

"One of the other guests gave it to me when I told him my mother's mother was Italian. I only took it to be friendly."

I'd never gone into family history with Hasty, and people had all kinds of grannies. Still, the Italian connection was unexpected. "Leo Di Giovanni — was that this guest's name?"

"Exactly. He said he understood that mixed marriages happened in the past, but that this tragedy of Italians diluting their blood was now going to stop. It's part of the message he's carrying to Little Italies all over North America. New York, Montreal, Ottawa, Chicago, Toronto — wherever his export business takes him. He said the Italian government sees all these emigrant communities as colonies and needs them as a matter of patriotic duty to stay pure and strong. He doesn't like Italian shops being sold to non-Italians either."

"Any of that mean anything to you?" I asked.

"Golly no. How could a mongrel like me believe in pure blood? But I do think Mussolini's the one great man of our age. Look at the discipline he's managed to instill in his country. He's chased out the Communists, abolished inheritance tax, preserved the monarchy, is making peace with the Vatican. Not to mention the improvement in the railways."

I was surprised to hear Hasty talk this way, and wondered at first if it was just idle chatter. But he seemed to be getting more and more wound up.

"Benito's balanced the budget, turned the telephones over to private ownership, trimmed the bureaucracy. So the business types are happy, but look at what he's done for the workers as well. Labour peace, no more strikes or lockouts, an eight-hour day. And this isn't just the Italian view. The man has admirers in the States and Britain too. Am I right, Paul? Tell me what you think."

"Hasty, I don't care who owns the telephones as long as they work. All that jawing about whose hands the means of production are in just makes my mind wander to where my next drink is coming from."

Hasty, stout lad, pointed to a dresser drawer where I found an unlabelled bottle containing two mouthfuls of a clear liquid that smelled slightly better than cleaning fluid.

"As a policeman, though," he persisted, "you must appreciate peace and order. The protection of private property and all that."

I took a sip and passed the bottle to my host. *As a policeman*, I was used to distillery whisky, but for bathtub gin this wasn't bad. I loosened my tie and hung my jacket on the doorknob.

. "I'll level with you, Hasty," I said. "For some of the detective sergeants in my department, the job of the police is to defend the rich against the poor. They'd have it that the people that wash behind their ears and have servants to dust their china ornaments are law-abiding and that criminals have dirt under their fingernails. My mind, on the other hand, is open to the possibility that ladies and gentlemen are every bit as larcenous as the people they give or don't give work to."

"But didn't the war teach us the value of disciplined, co-ordinated action? That's what Mussolini is applying to Italy today."

Here we go again, I thought. *The lessons of the war.*

"Look," I said. "You and I volunteered for the 48th Highlanders. We weren't conscripts. However bad things got in Flanders, I felt I'd made a choice to be there. Then, when the brass hats started calling for volunteers to raid German trenches and bring prisoners back for interrogation, I stepped forward again. Not because I was a hero, but —"

"Because you needed the thrill, from what I saw."

"No. Well, partly — but mainly because I wanted to feel I had some power over my own fate, that I wasn't just being tossed like a piece of meat into the grinder. Do you see?"

Hasty said he more or less did.

"Then take the next step," I urged him. "If a person likes to choose, even within narrow limits, then that person has to be a democrat. I want to live in a country where you can speak for or against the government without getting your head broken, and where you can vote for or against the government in a free election. Those are choices I'm hearing your Mussolini doesn't let people make, so don't expect me to be singing his praises. Or Comrade Stalin's either, for that matter. And as for running a country like an army — if I didn't expect a better life in peacetime than wartime, I'd slit my throat."

"You make it sound so gloomy, PS, when it needn't be at all." Hastings MacDermid's tall face lit up like a beacon. "Democracy was all very well in its day, but I'm wondering if there isn't something newer and shinier on the horizon."

By the time we'd been around the course a few more times, Hasty suggesting democracy was obsolete and me arguing it had barely even been tried yet, the hour was getting late. So late that when I left him and knocked on the door of Room 38 it seemed odd that Leo Di Giovanni wasn't in yet.

I met him coming up the stairs, however. He would have been impossible to pass. He was wide-shouldered and the way he swung his arms as he climbed made him wider still. A tight jaw combined with a project-ing chin expressed determination, and the tilt of his head added a note of arrogance, but he also looked pleased with himself. His tan suit jacket flapped open, his tie was loose, and when he reached the landing where I stood I noticed an imprint of scarlet lipstick at the corner of his mouth.

I identified myself.

"Not this *mafioso* business again." Di Giovanni clicked his tongue reprovingly. "Understand the *Duce* is making war on these thugs in the south. They are not tolerated in the new Italy."

"From what I hear, they're in good company." I could see he wanted to give me an earful. "Say, can we talk in your room? We don't want to disturb the other guests."

He let me in without offering me a seat. I took the only chair. I thought if I could goad him a little I might catch him off guard.

"I understand you've been stirring up hostility between Italians and non-Italians," I said. "Telling your people not to marry or sell their shops to outsiders."

"What law am I breaking? Canada is a free country, no?"

"Freer than Italy, it seems. What business did you have with the woman in Room 29?"

"Man-woman business."

"She turned you down."

Di Giovanni flushed. "The other way if anything." He struggled to recover his self-satisfaction. "No matter," he said, forcing a smile. "In a city as big as this one, there are always other women."

"What help did you give to the man that attacked her?"

"Attacking a woman is cowardly. Teaching a policeman manners, *invece* — that has it's place."

I grinned up at him. "What were you doing out on the fire escape Friday morning?"

"I didn't go there."

The surprised, prompt way the words popped out of his belligerent mouth told me I'd got what I'd come for, so I called it a night.

Chapter 8

LUCY'S STRATEGY FOR ENGLAND had failed. For the United States, she tried something different.

Many Poles had emigrated from their divided and occupied country before the war. A large portion had gone to America. A shipboard acquaintance named Robak told her that some of these had now returned or contemplated returning to their motherland, newly re-established as a free and independent state by the Treaty of Versailles. To Lucy, this suggested that Polish Americans would take her warning seriously. Their politics should be less isolationist than those of Americans with other roots. Furthermore, Lucy feared that she was a marked woman since her interview with the English agents. They might already have warned their U.S. counterparts to arrest a woman of her appearance with her sort of çockeyed tales to tell. Or if Harry North were a Soviet agent, he could advise his American comrades to kill her. Better then for her to remain underground and let leaders of the Polish community convey her photographs to Washington.

Lucy didn't take Mr. Robak into her confidence, but told him she wished to interview respected Polish Americans for a magazine article. Who should she speak to?

Respected? Robak snorted. Well, then: she certainly didn't want to have anything to do with *him*. Two gold teeth showed when he smiled. He was a dapper little man of sixty or so with wavy, grey hair brushed back and a twinkle in his eye. He told her he was a restaurateur in Greenpoint, Brooklyn, but hinted he might be a bootlegger as well. As for Poles in America, they ran the gamut from cavalry officers to cosmetics tycoons. Pulaski had been dead for 150 years and Max Factor lived in Hollywood, but there were some locals Lucy should have a word with. Her first call should be on Nick Mazur, head of the polling division of *Public Voice* magazine. Influential? You bet. Their office was in the Woolworth Building. Then Lucy could try Bruce Bielaski, for seven years head of the Bureau of Investigation, a U.S. federal police force. Bielaski was out of that now, but was working in New York City as a prohibition agent. Undercover and very hush-hush, but Robak happened to know that Bielaski was running a decoy speakeasy. He wrote the address out for her. Would he, Lucy asked, go there with her? Not on her life! Robak seemed to think this the joke of the century.

The other subject on which Lucy would have liked to pick her fellow passengers' brains was how easy it was for Scotland Yard to get access to the passenger lists of United States ships sailing from U.K. ports. She was afraid, however, that such an enquiry would attract suspicion, and so was left to her own speculations. She'd met the ship's chief Marconi officer, a sharp-eyed young man named Meyer, who seemed always to be hurrying somewhere. Whenever they passed on deck, he touched his cap politely. But something in the glances he shot her made her wonder what news his radio set had just pulled out of the ether and whether he was at that very moment speeding to warn the captain that the passenger calling herself Edna Salisbury was not what she seemed.

What she was unprepared for was herself to be the recipient of a Marconigram. The sealed envelope had been slipped under her stateroom door and was waiting for her that last night when she returned from the salon, her handbag bulging with her winnings. Lucy pried up the flap and read this brief message on the flimsy yellow form:

> *Sorry I missed seeing you off. Have a*
> *wonderful trip.*
>
> Mother

In any language, there was no word more distressing to her than the one with which this message was signed. She saw seated at the parlour piano a woman with knitted eyebrows and a nagging cough, sad even before losing one child to Russia and another to war.

A woman whose gentle touch had so soothed Lucy as an infant and so irked her as an adolescent, when gentleness had seemed tantamount to resignation.

Lucy wiped her nose with the back of her hand. Someone knew how to hit where it hurt.

London was the name, printed in block letters, filling the form's Office of Origin box — but she couldn't imagine that this cruel fake wire represented British Government style. It had to be Harry, his double-agent status now beyond doubt. Lucy felt she could stop fearing an arrest in New York. That wasn't the Soviet game. A woman alone on the pier would be much easier to snatch than one escorted by police into custody. All OGPU needed to know was which boat their thugs should meet, then get a passenger to point her out. One of last night's sore losers would gladly do so even if, especially if, he or she suspected no good to Lucy was intended. And the devil of it was that she couldn't change her appearance before she got her — Edna's — passport stamped.

She hurried up to the Marconi office where Meyer, despite the lateness of the hour, was still on duty. She showed him the message and told him it was not for her. Meyer impaled her with one of his looks. Was her name not Edna Salisbury? Then there was no mistake. Meyer had transcribed the words himself, address, body, and signature, just as they had been sent. Lucy asked what would have happened if there had been no such passenger aboard. Meyer said he would then have returned a message to that effect. Could Meyer not now return such a message, seeing as *this* — Lucy waved the form — was clearly not for her? Meyer said no. Not if her name was Edna Salisbury.

On Wednesday, September 1, as *Luxuria* was being piloted through the Ambrose Channel and the Narrows towards her North River berth, Lucy located Mr. Robak. She confessed to having passed an anxious night. Silly of her, of course — but she wondered if he'd mind if they went ashore together and shared a cab as far as the Manhattan YWCA. She'd pay for it naturally. Robak kissed her hand in the most gallant Polish style. It was not his practice, he said, to let ladies pay. Still, he thought he might make an exception today, knowing how well she could afford it. The whole ship was abuzz with the killing Miss Salisbury had made last night.

Lucy could have done with less notoriety and wished she'd left the poker table an hour sooner. Her wish doubled in strength when she returned to her cabin for the last time and found her stewardess waiting to be generously thanked.

Travelling first-class had been the only way of securing the privacy necessary to maintain the disguise Lucy's alias required. To have Cora Lynch dancing attendance on her at all hours would have defeated that purpose entirely. Accordingly, the pampering it was Cora's job to provide had had to be declined on almost every occasion. In Cora's decade and a half of ocean liner experience, the easiest passengers were usually those that brought aboard their own ladies' maids, but here was Miss Salisbury without a servant to her name and yet never in need of help dressing or undressing, never wanting a cup of tea or chocolate brought to her in bed. On the sixth day, Lucy had ripped a seam in one of her hideous shirtwaists on purpose, just to give the stewardess some mending to do.

Now Cora looked askance at the twenty-dollar bill Lucy shoved into her hand. From a pocket of her black dress she produced a packet of the mortician's wax Lucy used to build her Edna nose. Strange thing to find under Miss Salisbury's bed, wasn't it? Or perhaps not; Cora guessed professional card sharps had to keep changing their appearance. It wouldn't do to become too well known by their marks — or by the shipping companies if it came to that. Cora wondered aloud what a little packet like this might be worth.

If Lucy hadn't made an arrangement with Mr. Robak, she might have told Cora to go ahead and have her arrested. As it was, she handed the stewardess a wad of bills and left her to count them.

Passengers had by now assembled in the lounge. Immigration officers were stamping passports and handing out landing cards. Lucy was processed without a hiccup.

The sun burned bright. The sky resembled a vivid blue canopy onto which small, white clouds had been stitched at wide intervals. It was a glorious summer's morning on which to be walking down the gangplank on Robak's arm. As a bodyguard, he was rather small and elderly, but in his inside jacket pocket there was a bulge Lucy's practised eye told her was a handgun. She figured that if he were slow to reach for it in a crisis she'd help herself.

She tensed at the sight of two large men in dark suits standing between the foot of the gangplank and the customs shed. At her side, Robak sighed and told her to relax: they were there for him, not her. Name, arrest for various liquor offences, surrender of any firearms — it all passed in the blink of an eye. Just before he was led away, Robak expressed regret that he wasn't going to be able to take that taxi ride with Lucy after all. But she mustn't worry. She'd be safe in New York.

Chapter 9

WHY DID THE CHICKEN cross the road? Why did Lucy cross the pond?

These were the great issues with which the evening of Sunday, September 5 found me grappling. I was lying on my back on my bed in my stuffy room, staring at the spider webs in a corner of the ceiling. The heat wave showed no signs of ending, but I was still dressed because I wasn't sure that my thirst would not drive me out to look for someone that would give me a drink on credit. I still had one good gulp of rye whisky behind the encyclopedias, but I couldn't stand the thought of running out entirely.

The subject on which I'd have welcomed a thought was this: if pursuit by John Doe, dressed by a New York City department store, had driven Lucy out of the States, what had driven her in? What had made it worth her while to tamper with Edna Salisbury's passport in such a way as to allow her to leave England for America? The money in her girdle was dollars, not pounds. I played around with Sanderson's organized crime hypothesis. Perhaps on the other side of the Atlantic Lucy had got involved with an international gang and stolen from them — what? — jewellery or drugs, which she had then sold in the U.S. Three hundred dollars didn't seem enough to justify such a long-range vendetta. Maybe, though, it was a matter of principle — that or the cash found in Lucy's girdle was only part of the proceeds. The mobs Di Giovanni claimed Mussolini was warring with in Calabria or Sicily might have such an extensive reach. I wondered if there were others.

Perhaps I should be thinking of the Fascists themselves as a mob. They certainly played rough. Hotel guest Leo Di Giovanni, if not a party member, was a sympathizer — enough of one to be handing out lapel pins. And Di Giovanni was the one hotel guest that admitted to having seen Lucy. There was no evidence Lucy had ever been to Italy, but possibly she had run afoul of Fascist sympathizers in Great Britain.

I got no farther when there was a knock on my door, strong, peremptory, masculine. I was wary, though. Since Dot had started making a pest of herself, she had knocked in a different style each time, hoping to catch me off guard. I couldn't think why the little shopgirl was stuck on a man of my thirty-four years, except that she believed in the glamour of detective work. At the drugstore, I'd once caught her reading *The Mysterious Affair at* ... wherever. Try convincing a fan of those books that most affairs aren't mysterious — and that those that are exasperate more often than they thrill. Like this Mills bomb business. The knock was repeated. I couldn't pretend not to be home tonight as my light could be seen under the ill-fitting door.

"Who's there?"

More knocking.

My door had no peephole. I'd often thought I should speak to the landlord about that. Not that it mattered in this case, for by now I knew it was Dot. Anyone else would have said something. She must have reached the same conclusion.

"Featherstone Drugs delivery," she declared ringingly. "I have a quart."

Guilty as I was of flouting the Ontario Temperance Act, I'd never sunk to getting a doctor's prescription for whisky sold through a drug store. And I didn't want my neighbours thinking I had. I slid back the bolt.

The little monkey had the decency not to make her smile too triumphal. She was wearing a tennis dress and tapped me on the arm with her racquet by way of greeting. She knew I didn't like her cozying up.

"Where's the quart?" I asked.

She took a bottle of Seagram's out of her shoulder bag. It was only a mickey.

"And the other half?"

"I exaggerated. Don't look so glum. If I were a drinking woman, you'd have to share."

"If you were a *woman* instead of a fifteen-year-old kid —"

"For Pete's sake, Paul! You're a broken record." The girl blew a raspberry in my direction then jumped up on the end of the bed and sat there swinging her legs, ignoring me. Her yellow bangs were sticking in spikes to her damp forehead. Eventually, she rolled her blue eyes in my direction. "Where did you get the idea I'm fifteen?"

"Maybe from seeing you roller skating around the schoolyard last June." I didn't want to get into the question of her curves or lack thereof.

"Skating's good exercise. I don't think that's it at all. You figure I'm a kid because I'm short, and even more because I'm skinny. If you read your newspaper right through, Mr. Detective, instead of just the crime stories, you'd know my shape is very voguish right now. In fact — coveted." She sounded childishly proud at having got the word out.

"Show me your birth certificate," I said.

"No, damn you. That's humiliating."

"You admit you exaggerate."

"Not about important things." Then she sniffed and seemed to decide I wasn't worth glaring at. "Mind if I smoke?"

"I do mind. And it's bad for your complexion."

She had the skin artists paint on angels, as smooth and unblemished as a cloudless sky. It wasn't that I didn't find Dot attractive. With or without curves, in three or four years she'd be a knockout. Then — ah, nuts, I'd still be too old for her.

"I guess I'd better rough my skin up a bit to help me look my age. I'll smoke more."

"Dottie, I'm going to ask you to leave now. Take the mickey with you; I can't pay you for it."

"It's a present."

"I'll reimburse you later."

"Can I finish my cigarette first?" She made a show of puffing on her Player's more vigorously; well before it was finished, she gave up and took it into the kitchenette alcove, where I could hear her drowning it in the sink. "So do you have a big case you're working on tonight, Paul? Say, what about the Beaconsfield Hotel? That's just down the road. I'll bet you have some hot ideas on that."

"You'll lose." I held the hall door open for her.

"Here's an idea you can have for free. I say that sap was a spurned admirer of the chippie in Room 29, and he blew himself up outside her door just to show her how much he cared. And when — too late — she realized what a true heart she'd trampled on, she ran away to join him in death. You'll find her waterlogged body on the bed of the Don River. Or possibly the Humber." She elbowed my ribs on the way out. "Abyssinia!"

I closed the door after her, put the mickey in the usual place, and lay down again to think. I must have dozed off a bit, because my ideas stopped making sense. I saw Dot playing tennis against some gangster, with a hand grenade in place of a ball. Then from off the court came the rat-tat-tat of machine gun fire in long, repeated bursts.

I came to to find that my door was again being knocked at. How was I ever going to get through to that kid, I wondered. Send her to her room without supper? Well, this time I wasn't letting her in, no matter what tosh she hollered. It was two a.m. for crying out loud.

Despite having put me in mind of gunfire, the knocks this time were low and gentle, meant to be heard only by me. This time when the knocking stopped another noise started, a scratching at the keyhole. I sat up smartly. Someone was picking my lock.

This was someone I wanted to meet, though perhaps not unarmed. While not big on war souvenirs, I kept a trench knife in the bottom of a dresser drawer. Noiselessly I retrieved the weapon — a nasty combination of dagger and brass knuckles — from under my winter woollens. Slipping the fingers of my right hand through the finger holes, I gripped the handle so that the double-edged blade pointed down. I reached the door just in time to see the handle turn. The picker had opened the lock, but the door was still held by the bolt. This I threw back with my knife hand and in one motion swept the door open with my left, ready to strike.

It was Lucy. Surprised as I was to see her, she was no less surprised at my threatening appearance. As she stepped back, I advanced, the knife point turned away from her, and got my arm around her waist. I bundled her into my apartment and closed the door, standing with my back to it. She was swathed from knees to chin in a new cocoa brown raincoat. A matching hat hid almost all her hair. Both coat and hat were dry, and no rain was forecast, so I assumed she was got up this way as a disguise. All the same, I had no trouble recognizing the pale grey eyes, pocked cheeks, arrow-straight nose, and all the other features I'd described so often in my search for her.

"You must be hot," I said. "Give me your coat. Have a seat." I used a lot of gestures, ending up by pointing to my one armchair. I figured I was going to have to park her in a police lockup and find someone familiar with Slavic languages before we could have much of a conversation. But now that I had her cornered I didn't see any harm in taking a moment for us to catch our breaths before I arrested her for the assault on Daisy Bennett.

"Someone is following me here," she said, her voice low in her throat.

"You speak English." The surprises kept piling up.

"We cannot stay in this room. I am fearing another bomb. Bigger this time." She lingered somehow over the letter *s*, and her *th* came out *d* — *diss room, diss time.*

"And what if they have guns and would be just as happy shooting you instead?"

She said *dat* was possible.

"Then walking out into the street or alley isn't safe either." I thought fast. "We'll wait in the basement till it gets light."

"Yes?"

"We'll be safe there even if they blow up this whole apartment."

She nodded. "We go now."

"In a moment."

I'd just had another idea. Every now and then a salesman makes the rounds of police forces with a new piece of equipment. In June, some johnny from the

Protective Garment Corp. came peddling bulletproof vests. The department wasn't buying, but he gave me one as a reward for shooting at his cotton-padded chest. So, although I'd had no call to put this fashion item on since, I thought it worth digging out of the back of my closet.

"Take off your raincoat a minute so we can get this on you."

She shook her head.

"Believe me, Lucy. I've seen this vest stop a .38 bullet from less than ten feet."

"In bathroom," she said. "I put on."

"It'll be easier if I tighten the straps." There were two to fasten under each arm, tricky till you got the hang of them. But I saw she was blushing. I guessed she'd discarded Miss Bennett's ill-fitting nursing uniform. Unfortunately, the suitcase with Lucy's own clothes was at HQ. "Perhaps you're between wardrobes," I said. "Would these be of use to you?"

I handed her a pullover sports shirt and some old trousers of mine. She went into my bathroom and came out wearing them, after a fashion. It took her no longer to dress than it took me to find and put on my shoes. We got the vest on her and all the straps tightened and her raincoat back in place before the trousers fell down. She stepped out of them, and they remained on the floor when we left. I took only Lucy, my room key, and my knife.

My apartment was on the building's third floor, the highest and hottest. We could feel the temperature falling as we crept down to the second, the first, and at last the basement — mouldy-smelling on this humid night. I paused at the foot of the stairs to whisper in Lucy's ear.

"The furnace room — no one goes there this time of year."

She nodded. The corridor was dimly lit by widely spaced fifteen-watt bulbs. To reach the furnace room we had to get down to the end and around a corner to the right. I took Lucy's hand and stole forward.

No plan is perfect. One hitch in mine was the blind corner between us and our refuge. Another now stared me in the face. Straight ahead, at the elbow, was an outside door. It opened into an exterior concrete stairwell, accessible from the alley. One thing in our favour: no one could be waiting and watching us from behind that door. Its wire-reinforced window had been covered with brown paper, for reasons best known to the superintendent. He was a security-conscious older man, who I believed could be trusted to keep every way into the building locked — although, as tonight had already demonstrated, the locks weren't up to much. I figured that, while an attacker could get in this way, odds were we'd make it to safety before one did.

At the corner, I dropped Lucy's hand for a moment to peer around into the next stretch of hall. All clear. As I stepped into it, however, I heard the outside door open behind me. I spun around. On the instant, a deafening detonation. Lucy dropped to the floor — whether defensively or because she'd been hit I had no time to find out. Before he could get off a second shot, I stepped into the man with the pistol, my left hand closing over the wrist of his right hand, forcing the aim of his revolver low and wide. With all the strength in my right arm I swung my trench knife backhand into the gunman's face. He staggered but kept his grip on the gun.

"Drop it," I snarled.

I expected him to cover his face with his left hand, but I felt it clamp instead around my throat, forcing my head back. As long as he held his pistol I dared not let go his wrist. With the backward pressure on my throat I needed both feet for balance, so kicking was out. I still had my knife, though now — because of the angle of my head — I was stabbing blind. I yanked his right arm closer and buried the blade in it. Only then did I hear the pistol clatter to the concrete. I was at last able to free my left hand for a punch to the man's gut. That left him winded, giving me time to break his grip on my throat. I used both hands for the job, leaving the knife where I'd stuck it. Better balanced, I got a leg forward and over it threw him to the ground.

"Lucy," I called without chancing a look. "Are you hurt? Get the gun if you can. *You*, mister —" Suddenly I recognized him: Room 33 at the Beaconsfield, with easy access to the fire escape — multiple copies of Soviet tracts — weapons training courtesy of the Princess Louise Fusiliers. Still, who would have thought the meek typesetter would have had so much fight in him? "Ewart, you stay down."

I stood on his arm and grabbed the knife with both hands to pull it out, but when blood started pumping from the wound, I realized I'd severed an artery.

"Go on, take it," he gasped.

I didn't, though. Ewart's chances of surviving to be questioned would be better if I left the blade where it was. He was bleeding also, but less dangerously, from a hole in his cheek.

Finally I risked a glance over my shoulder. The revolver was still on the floor where it had fallen. Lucy had vanished.

I picked up the gun, a hammerless Smith and Wesson with bullets still in the cylinder, and covered Ewart with it. He was pulling up the top of his shirt. I guessed he wanted to make a pad to hold over the face wound. Too late I realized he was biting down on a button. I moved to scoop it out of his mouth, but before I could get my fingers in between his teeth, spasms were racking his body. They ended soon enough. Next I knew Ewart's jaw had locked up tight, his lips drawn back into a rictus. He must have understood I wasn't going to let him bleed to death. In any case, the cyanide was faster.

Chapter 10

I DID MY BEST to distract myself with routine and paperwork the rest of the night. Everyone was unhappy with me, starting with the building superintendent and ending with myself.

The former, who had slept through the firing of a .32 calibre pistol beneath his bedroom, wondered why I'd woken him up to tell him not to clean the basement corridor, something he'd had no intention of doing at that hour anyway. And having a resident policeman in the building was all very well, but why did I have to bring my work home? Parkdale Station grumbled at my request for a police photographer at that ungodly hour, and on a holiday Monday to boot. The ambulance men that came to transport Ewart's remains to Grace Hospital grumbled at me for having interrupted their game of spit in the ocean. I knew the keeper of the petty cash box at HQ would grumble at me if I expected to be reimbursed for my taxi ride downtown, even though the Queen streetcar wasn't running on Labour Day at four in the morning. I wasn't the world's fastest typist and was still pecking out my report on one of the department's battered Underwoods at eight thirty when Inspector Sanderson sailed in freshly shaved and not yet enveloped in pipe smoke. Why he had no better place than HQ to spend the last day of the long weekend I didn't know and didn't ask. When he heard what the Sam Hill I was up to at this hour, he gathered me into his office and grumbled at me for letting Lucy out of my clutches. Then he told me I wasn't fit to be seen in any self-respecting police office and sent me home to sleep for eight hours. I could report back to him that night at six. By then he'd have read my typescript.

How like the inspector not to go overboard and give me the whole day off! But I had to hand it to him — how like him also to stay late himself!

I'll admit I was rattled by Ewart's attack. Duty-bound to leave my trench knife in evidence storage at HQ, I unlocked a desk drawer I rarely go into. My service revolver and its shoulder rig, supposed to be worn only by detectives on duty, went home with me that morning. A box of ammunition too.

The streetcars were running now, and the ride out Queen West gave me time to mull over where I'd slipped up. Lucy's disappearance was unfortunate, but not the worst of it. In the first place, I was sure she'd left under her own steam, not been snatched. Busy as I was with Ewart, I'm sure I'd have noticed the approach of any of his comrades behind me. This mattered to me because it had looked as if Ewart's shot had been right on target.

A miss would have left a bullet and some scarring of the corridor walls. I'd found no trace of either. Therefore, if Lucy had run away, it meant that Ewart's bullet had hit the vest and — as at the demonstration — the vest had done its job. A search with a strong flashlight turned up no drop of blood on floor, walls, or ceiling. I took some comfort also from the fact that Lucy had come to me of her own volition. I just hoped that her reason for doing so had not expired with the latest assailant and that she'd be back. I couldn't in any case have restrained Lucy and subdued Ewart at the same time.

Ewart had been a handful, and more. The man had fought like a tiger. My mind went back to the trench raids I'd gone out on during the war and to the ones our platoon had repelled. I'd done a good deal of hand-to-hand in Flanders, some of it against elite German regiments, but even these supermen would fall back in shock on getting a knife in the face. Maybe everyone, volunteers no less than conscripts, had been worn down by the rats and the mud, the stench and the sepsis, the poor rations and the sleepless nights. By 1917, in any case, nothing like the combat zeal of this Canadian Communist had animated even the most fanatical believers in *Gott mit uns*.

And then, once I had him, my sloppy policing had let Ewart escape questioning.

I just hadn't been ready for his fervour. Maybe I'd let myself be lulled by the *Socialism in one country* slogan. The words expressed a vision utterly opposed to the nightmare of world revolution that made our businessmen squeal with fear. One country, only one — Russia. Not countries all over Europe or here in North America. No hint of gunplay and suicide in a Toronto basement. Perhaps this new Soviet policy turn was a ruse, a lullaby to soothe our fears while the bloodbath was being prepared. Whatever the plan — whether this one-country stuff was on the level or not — I now had to assume the Communist International considered little Miss Lucy a fly in their ointment. A fly that had now cost the party at least two flycatchers.

Just before ten a.m., the car reached my stop. When I let myself into my apartment, she was lying on the bed, snoring lightly, her raincoat thrown on the armchair, the vest still strapped on over my jersey, and my baggy old trousers pulled primly back up around her waist. I could have gone to the police call box on the corner and arranged for a paddy wagon to come and pick her up. Against this course of action was my reluctance to entrust her to anyone but myself. What's more, I reckoned I'd earned the right to be the first to question her. I'd nursed her. I'd beaten the bushes for her. And after playing hard to get, the rare bird had chosen *my* nest to land in. Naturally, I was possessive. Most of all, though, I was too dog tired to do much of anything.

I slipped off my shoes, padded into the kitchen, and buried the key to Rutherford's handcuffs in a box of cornflakes. I examined the cuffs to make sure I understood how they functioned. They could be carried closed without being locked, as indeed they had been carried in the constable's pouch before Lucy lifted them — and in my pocket since their removal from Benny's wrists. A lock release button on the outside of each bracelet had to be depressed before closing the cuffs would lock them.

I returned to the bedroom and locked one cuff around the sleeping woman's right wrist, the other around my left.

Lucy groaned and blinked at me. "What is this?" She tugged and pulled my hand up with hers in front of her face.

"Nothing," I said. "Go to sleep."

She did, and for once I was able to follow her.

Some hours later I felt my wrist being tugged — gently, as if by accident. She was trying not to wake me. Night had come again, and it was too dark for me to see what she was doing. My right hand found the switch for the bedside lamp. Lucy's right wrist was bleeding, especially over the bump.

"Bones too big," she explained with a sigh.

"You want to run away again?" I asked.

"Only to WC."

My bathroom hugged the corridor wall of the apartment, with no window and a vent shaft too narrow for her to crawl out through.

"Come into the kitchen first."

She looked at me as if I were cracked, but went along. The kitchenette took up the space between the bathroom and the outside wall. Like the rest of the apartment, it had many years ago been painted a dull ochre shade that was darkening with time. Two of the three low-wattage bulbs in the ceiling fixture were burned out, and the kitchen window — which faced another dark apartment block — was too far back from Queen to catch any of the street lighting. After nightfall, I navigated the alcove raccoon-style, mostly by touch. I got my paw into the cereal box and eventually brought it out with the key. Once we were detached, I let Lucy help herself to a fresh towel from the icebox, which held all my linens. She was surprised to find it warm. I explained that I'd discontinued ice deliveries, thinking I'd buy an electric refrigerator, but hadn't yet managed to save enough. Cold storage would have been nice in this heat. Not being much of a beer drinker, though, I found I could get by without.

"Do you have here some dinner?" she asked when she came out of the bathroom. "For trousers I must be fatter."

I found a safety pin in my bachelor sewing kit and nipped the waist in for her. She wasn't ticklish; we both took the business in course. All the clothes (and lack of clothes) rigmarole we'd been through had reminded me some time earlier that Lucy was not just a fugitive but a woman. I have to say, though, the new line made her look more feminine.

"Not afraid of explosions if we stay?" I said, keeping my voice flat.

"This time I was not followed."

I let my hand rest on her shoulder and looked into those distant grey eyes of hers. "Why are they trying to kill you, Lucy?"

"This is why I am coming to you. You must help me send a message to the United States President or, even better, King of England. They, the others, will do anything to stop me."

Now *I* looked at her as if *she* were off her head.

"You don't believe me," she sighed. "I will make you, but it will take time. We eat first."

"First," I corrected, "I'm putting a dressing on that wrist. Then, if you're good, I'll let you cook."

I'd just got a Band-Aid on when heavy boots clopped down the corridor and the door started rattling with thick-knuckled knocks. I put my finger to my lips. Lucy nodded. We both stood where we were.

"It's Constable Rutherford, Sergeant."

I didn't doubt it: the gravelly bass-baritone rang true, even more so the spirit — parade-ground correctness seasoned with put-upon impatience.

Rutherford knocked again, less resolutely. "Inspector Sanderson phoned Parkdale station and asked someone to come out here. He wants to see you at City Hall." Shuffling of feet. "Your light's on, so I presume you're home. Can you hear me, Sergeant?"

Lucy and I stayed quiet. Presently we heard a sound like paper ripping. A page from a police notebook with Sanderson's message pencilled in block capitals slid in under my door. I could almost hear Rutherford sigh as he turned to leave.

"Are you going?" Lucy asked once the clop of the constable's boots had faded off down the hall.

"Tomorrow." I figured by then I'd have something to report.

"What will they do to you?"

She looked so serious I had to laugh. Perhaps she was thinking of Soviet-style punishments — or maybe she was just afraid I'd be taken off the case and she'd have to start from scratch with some other detective.

"Try to starve me into submission," I said. "Let's have dinner."

She boiled some potatoes. I opened a tin of salmon and a tin of peas to go with them. While they were heating, I pulled the scarred drop-leaf table out from the window and opened it up, placing my dining room chair and kitchen chair to either side. Whatever I did, I never let Lucy get between me and the door to the corridor. Although she wouldn't start her long story, I tried to clear up a couple of details while we ate. It impressed me that she'd located the Reference Library and looked up my address in a city directory. As for the lock picks —

"Won in a card game with some Polish guys," she explained around a mouthful of potatoes. "I should have won money for clothes, but it was dishonest game."

"What about the rain gear — coat and hat?"

"Them I got before, on Friday afternoon. I buy on time, with first payment of fifty cents. The young man in the shop believed a nurse from Western Hospital would be honest to pay what more. And it maybe helped that my dress was very tight."

You hear a lot of accents in Toronto without thinking much about them, but that throaty Slavic voice of hers was growing on me. She spoke in all simplicity of gambling and burglary tools, and now of deploying a little sex appeal to work a con, while at the other end of her range she could carry off the straitlaced Edna Salisbury rôle. Any chump sweet on her would be in for a hell of a ride. I was happy enough just listening.

"You are thinking I stole from the skinny sister, but I left more money in the hospital."

"I suppose you charmed Constable Rutherford out of his handcuffs as well," I said.

"I demonstrate: you are policeman sitting beside my bed." She pointed to me, then drew her hands together in the air. "So he understands what I want; he closes curtains around my bed. Then to thank him ..." She beckoned me closer. I moved my chair next to hers and her arms went around me. She pressed her cheek to mine. It was a hug made to measure for a constable of Rutherford's age and prospects, and I enjoyed every second of it, even while my right hand was intercepting her left in the side pocket of my jacket. "Yes," she said, "but you are a sergeant and clever. You know, what is more, that Lucy is not only poor woman that got hit on the head, but a strangler and a thief."

"Don't forget picklock and vamp."

"And then before he can see them," she said, resuming her charade, "handcuffs go under the bed-clothes. I push him away. I yawn. I am sleepy now." Her hands shooed me back. "Your constable says if I would sleep, maybe he would go out to eat something. I don't let him see I understand, because sometimes it is more useful not to understand English and to speak with body. And now my body says how tired it is and tells policeman it's safe for leaving his post."

"Still," I said, squashing the last peas on my plate and licking them off my fork, "English is not your first language; I assume Lucy is not your real name."

"Svetlana is my Russian name, but I am not Russian. Lucja, which means same as Svetlana, is my Polish name. Lucja Grudzinska. Close enough to Lucy, don't you think?"

"So you speak Polish, Russian, German —"

"All better than English. I had aunts and uncles in Prussian part of Poland. I think you were in war fighting against Germans, taking some prisoner. I heard you say *Hände hoch*. Is it your belief that German soldiers surrender easily?"

After the Ewart business, I'd expected her to be talking about the long arm of Russian communism. "Germans? You have to surprise them — no walk in the park."

"Nice expression. But next time, *they* may be surprising *you*: this is my message for the West. Do you have vodka?"

"There's whisky behind the encyclopedias, glasses in the kitchen."

"Behind?" She walked over to the shelf.

"Not the Gs, further left."

"I want to see first what your encyclopedia says about Germany. Versailles Treaty forbids them to have warplanes, correct?" She pulled a volume off the shelf and leafed through till she found the article. "Listen: 'A new inter-Allied aeronautical committee of guarantee ...'"

"Take a deep breath," I advised.

"This committee 'receives lists of all German work-shops in which flying material is manufactured, of machines, and of pilots and sees that the provisions of the agreement are not infringed.' Do you believe this?"

I said that I did. That sure, sometimes there were slip-ups, but that these days the world was jogging along no worse than usual. For my pains, Lucy told me I was a baby.

"The guy that tried to kill you this morning," I pointed out, "was a Nova Scotia born Scots-Canadian Communist, not a German warmonger."

"He talked to you?" Lucy's eyebrows went up.

"No, he choked on a shirt button before he could be questioned."

"You have not to worry about that with me. I am the girl without buttons."

"Say, I thought you were getting us a drink."

Lucy shuffled my library around until she found the rye, then banged around the kitchen until she found something to put it in. She emptied the old mickey into one glass and poured the same amount from the new mickey into another.

"I know all about shirt-button suicide pills," she informed me. "Until one month ago, I belonged to the Soviet Russian secret police."

"Sure you did."

"Yes, just like my countryman Felix Dzerzhinsky, except that he was the tsar of OGPU and I foot soldier. *Na zdrowie!* Cheers!"

"What happened to him?" The only Felix *I* knew was a cartoon cat with black fur.

"Felix escaped by fatal heart attack — no tears for him, please; he still believed. Me, I felt fooled and betrayed. I got out by crawling on my stomach through the Pripet Marshes. That's one of two big reasons why they must kill me. No one is permitted to leave OGPU. In fact, no one is permitted to leave Russia, but for that they would not chase me so far."

"You want me to ask you the other big reason," I said.

"The other big reason is that I have evidence that USSR is secretly helping Germany prepare the next war."

If the conversation had been spooling out in an interrogation room at HQ, I'd have been doing my damnedest to drag the professed secret policewoman back to earth. Or maybe have been ringing for a psychologist. I'd heard from one such that a person's talent for day-to-day survival was no guarantee she was free of paranoid delusions. But in my own bed-sitter with a drink in my hand and no one looking over my shoulder, I felt I had time to see if Lucy and reason truly had parted company. Besides, this *next war* delusion was familiar to me; I'd come close to sharing it.

Except that I couldn't see how the Russians fit in.

"Communists helping capitalists?" I said. "Isn't that like oil mixing with water? Cats helping dogs?"

"Today's Politburo cares nothing for international Communism. These two countries both hate Versailles Treaty. It's enough."

"The last war put a check on German militarism,"

I said. "Now before you say I'm all wet, let me tell you I didn't think so at first."

I hadn't thought so on the morning of November 11, 1918, when our battalion stood holding our breaths in the Grande Place in Somain, the main square of a small French town only twenty-five miles east of Vimy. On the stroke of eleven a.m., the mad rejoicing began. French families broke out the wine they'd hidden from the enemy. Hasty MacDermid sang Gilbert and Sullivan songs from the church bell tower. I was among the minority that couldn't join in. It was as if, for the few of us, our minds were locked into a stance of attention. Perhaps I was still anticipating a postscript.

For the rest of November we marched east across a scarred and mutilated Belgium to occupy the German city of Cologne. The Armistice was still holding when in a driving rain I marched across the Rhine at the head of my platoon, and the Armistice held over the following weeks as impatience replaced elation among the men. You heard less of *The war is over; we made it through!* and more of *The war is over; when do we go home?* But armistice is not peace. I had no trouble remembering that the war was not over. In part because I kept remembering the faces of men in my platoon that had been killed — particularly the last one, a young private caught in the German wire and machine gunned at Canal du Nord. But mostly because, although I saw hungry and grieving families in Germany, their homes, schools, churches, and barns remained standing and intact, their fields uncratered by mines and shells. The devastation of the last four years was all behind us, in France and Belgium. I'd had a feeling the people we now lived among would never see the full cost of war or learn of it in other than the driest bookkeeping terms. Never, that is, until war broke out again.

"It's a funny thing, Lucy," I said. "Even in June 1919, when they made peace official in the Hall of Mirrors at Versailles, I had no confidence that we were done. Nothing changed for me until after the first Remembrance Day that November. People were summing up the year, and how trade was being re-established with Germany. Only then did I think we had a real likelihood of putting armed combat behind us. I think it more all the time. The League of Nations is working. Germany will soon be a member. And the Boche signed something at Locarno last year that makes war with France impossible."

Lucy had heard me out, her chin resting on one hand. Now she pushed a wavy lock of dark brown hair behind her ear and went on the attack.

"You see Weimar Republic admitted to the League of Nations and you think they want peace. *Absurd!* Peace in West, for now, maybe. Not in the East — not till they've had a bite of Poland. And even if some parts of the German government would want peace, the German military wants war. And illegally they are acquiring means to wage war. Listen."

Her story took the rest of the night. That's when I heard, for the first time and all at once, what I've already laid out in instalments. I haven't tried to set it down in her screwball English. Her inconsistencies made me think she'd forgotten how to speak rather than never known; for instance, she was capable when she thought about it of sticking *the* and *a* in where necessary, but was at excitable moments as stingy with them as if she were sending a telegram at a dollar a word.

How much of it did I believe? Her claims about this Lipetsk place were far-fetched and damn hard to swallow. There was little I could corroborate, naturally, but by going over what a witness says forwards and backwards, and testing whether it comes out the same every time, an experienced cop gets a sense of how things must have been. As regards facts as opposed to the language in which she retailed them, Lucy wasn't scattered or confused. She didn't contradict herself, and I never had the feeling she was improvising. If anything, her story came out too consistent, but then again she'd had hours on the road and on the seas to rehearse it. Pat didn't mean false.

I took it as evidence of trustworthiness that, while she didn't brag about her crimes, she didn't hide them either. She did claim she'd never killed or crippled anyone, and I had to call her on that. Partial strangulation — which she'd used last Friday on a young nurse here in town and, she said, on a milkmaid in Poland — was riskier than Lucy made it sound. Miscalculate the angle: you break a neck. Miscalculate the duration: your victim sinks into a coma or dies. Luckily for all concerned, Daisy Bennett was back on her feet, but how the deuce could we know that that Polish girl had fared as well? I bet Lucy hadn't hung around to see her victim recover.

At that, a shadow passed across Lucy's face, and vanished.

"You lead a soft life, Sergeant," she retorted. "You can afford such thoughts."

By four a.m., my place was cool enough that you could lift your glass without breaking out in a sweat. Lucy had stopped after three drinks. I'd lost count but was spinning this one out so as to leave a last ounce in the second mickey, just in case she changed her mind. She was sitting up on the bed with a pillow stuck between her and the headboard. I had the armchair pulled close to the window. A breeze had come up, enough to ruffle my curtains — stiff as they were with city dust and soot. Through the open window we heard from the direction of Queen Street a truck with a busted muffler rolling by, likely bringing produce from the Niagara fruit farms in to the Dominion store. When the engine noise faded, the peace of the night settled in again, a peace underlined rather than broken by the sighs and creaks of the settling apartment block.

I still had questions, of course, and after that last mouthful of rye I started in on them. "So did you get to Bruce Bielaski and get him stirred up?"

"Bielaski? No, not Mazur either. I had to leave town — I would say rather quickly — after I pushed Soviet agent off the world's tallest building."

"What was in that letter anyway?" I said, ignoring the cheesy teaser. "And did you still have the thirty-five millimetre negatives at this point?"

"I have them right here." She showed me her perfect smile.

She was not what you'd call a beautiful woman, except for certain features — her mouthful of even teeth among them. She knew the effect she was having on me. Though I couldn't help thinking she enjoyed flirting too much for someone that believed her country was on the chopping block. Then again, maybe it was just her European style, not in the least a sign of shallow feelings: I did have first-hand evidence that someone was trying to kill her. Most likely she thought I was the shallow one, in need of charming to keep me interested in German warplanes. Not too flattering. Any way I sliced it, I felt I had to suspect that smile.

"You mean right here in this room?" I asked, trying to look everywhere but at her. Failing.

"Right here in this mouth." She took out an upper dental plate attached to a number of teeth.

I started from my chair, grimacing involuntarily. Her face without the denture was old and witchlike.

"'Ight 'ere." Hollow-sounding, mutilated words.

The pink Vulcanite panel moulded to rest against the roof of her mouth separated into two layers. From between them she removed what looked like a waterproof envelope. The rye rose in my throat. Seeing my distress, she hastened to reassemble the plate and restore it to her mouth. Only then did she unseal the envelope. From it she took a short piece of photographic film.

"Have a look, Sergeant," she said gravely, her voice blessedly normal.

I could see nothing on the small negative except that the photographs appeared to be of documents.

"I told you Trigorin knocked out one tooth. I removed enough more to hold a denture in place. I knew a London dentist from my time there, someone I trusted, and he managed to make with hiding place. I never told British agents about my plate, so I was able to keep the photos even when my clothes were searched at the Ponds and my other things at my hostel room."

"You knocked out your own teeth?"

"Obviously. If Germany and Russia invade Poland, hundreds of thousands of my countrymen will lose their arms, legs, lives — things not so easy to replace. I disgust you, too bad."

"Okay."

"By *okay* you mean what? 'Calm down, you crazy woman'?"

"I mean okay," I said gently, intending not so much to calm her down as to tell her that — whatever reservations I'd had about her before — I now recognized how much those pictures meant to her. "What's in the letter?"

"Actually — now, I mean — I have no copy, but I memorized it every word. Do you want to write? While you find pen and paper, I'll put the negatives back. In bathroom, I think, would be more polite."

I wrote down what she recited when she came back, then went over it with her and cleaned it up, so it sounded more like English. Here's what I ended up with:

MOST SECRET
Kommandir A. S. Trigorin
Inspectorate of Aircraft, District G.
Voronezh, Russian SSR.
Instructions pertaining to the
German installation at Lipetsk

Comrade Commander,

You have already been briefed as to your regular duties regarding the inspection of Red Air Force facilities in District G. The presence in your district of a secret German flying school and test flight facility at Lipetsk necessitates these additional instructions.

Your comportment towards the German personnel at Lipetsk is to be cordial and discreet. Obtain the maximum information about German military strategy and equipment while revealing nothing of our own. In particular, find out as much as possible about German plans for the coming war against Poland. Reichswehr chief General Hans von Seeckt has assured the Revolutionary Military Council of the Soviet Union that obliteration of our common enemy Poland is the object of German rearmament. He has denied there can be any peaceful

*settlement of Polish-German issues
(Danzig, Upper Silesia, etc.). But the
General has so far revealed no time-
table for the invasion.*

Lucy said the senior officer that signed the letter,
a V.I. Kozlov, had apparently served with Trigorin in
the squadron of heavy bombers based in Jablonna
in 1915, for there was a handwritten postscript:
"Needless to say, Arkadi, we must be prepared to take
our share of the spoils. Who can forget the girls of
Warsaw?"

I was impressed — at the same time as the cop
in me was looking forward to getting enlarged photographic prints of the original Russian documents and
to having them independently translated.

"When that door to your room in the Beaconsfield
Hotel hit you on the head," I said, "you weren't really
knocked out. You just fainted."

"On back of my head, underneath my hair, I still
have a bump. Do you want to feel?"

"On *the* back of your head," I corrected. "If you had
been knocked out, chances are you wouldn't remember
anything about it — but you knew the man on the other
side of the door was trying to kill you. That's why you
ran away from the hospital. Who was he?"

"He followed me from New York — probably just
a party member. Not a trained assassin, that's for sure."

"Still, I wonder why he didn't throw that hand
grenade before it went off?"

"He did. I threw it back."

That shut me up for a good half minute. I tried to visualize Room 29 from the inside, a summer morning just heating up. The transom window open. A knock on the door, to bring Lucy closer to the blast. She goes to the door, not maybe to open it, but to listen. A grenade arcs in over the transom. She's been through the Russian Revolution and the Civil War; she knows what this is. Maybe she catches it before it hits the floor. Hot potato. Back she heaves it the way it came in, and before she can step back from the door, bam!

"You're a gutsy lady," I said at last. "You couldn't have known how long the fuse was or when he'd pulled the pin."

"All the chasing around was making me nervous — crazy, you might even say."

"I might. But for him to try a second throw was just plain stupid." I guessed it must have been one of those early Mills bombs with the seven second fuse — so long you lose track. They shortened the time to four seconds for the ones made later in the war. "Okay," I said, "better tell me the rest of the story, from the moment you arrived in New York and Robak got arrested."

"You said something about a walk in the park."

"It was just a turn of phrase."

"It would be nice, though. I could talk while we walk. Do you have a park?"

"Sure, High Park — the city's best, they say. But a park sounds like a swell place to get shot."

"Too bad. I wanted to see the sunrise."

"There'll be other sunrises, Lucy. Spill it."

Chapter 11

LUCY HAD HAD PLENTY of time on the boat to study Baedeker's guidebook, a map of the Interborough Rapid Transit Company's subway system, railway schedules, and various tourist pamphlets on the subject of New York, as well as to chat with passengers that knew the city. When she found herself alone on the pier, she decided her first job was to plan an emergency escape route, preferably to another jurisdiction. She already had a passport valid for the British Empire, and she knew that there were daily trains from Grand Central Terminal to Montreal and Toronto.

No subway station served the Chelsea Piers. From West Street, she took a cab to Grand Central, where she checked her suitcase and bought tickets for the next departures to each of Canada's two largest cities. In a cubicle of the women's room, she tucked the tickets along with emergency funds into a secret pocket of her underwear. She was watching for anyone trying to keep track of her movements, but couldn't tell if she were being followed. Just in case, she tried some of the elusive tricks she'd used in London. Two IRT lines served Grand Central, so it was easy to feint west, dodge back east and north, running between trains unencumbered by baggage, finally to end up three miles south at City Hall Park, face to face with the towering Woolworth Building.

She couldn't have missed it. If its height hadn't caught her eye, its brilliant whiteness in the midday sun would. It also had more carved decorations than a medieval cathedral, and that was just the outside. Inside the foyer, more money had been spent on mosaics, murals, marble, and other toys, which Lucy didn't stop to admire. She made straight for the directory and found that *Public Voice* magazine had its offices on the fourth floor. The first elevator she entered didn't stop there, the operator warned her, so she trotted across the lobby and slipped into one of the right cars just as the doors were closing. By now, if anyone had been tailing her, she was sure she'd lost him.

The lower floors of the building were U-shaped, with the base parallel to Broadway and the two wings extending back from the street to the west. The magazine took up the entire north wing. After asking around, Lucy arrived at the department of polls and surveys. A bronzed young man looking as if he'd just stepped off a magazine cover listened rather coolly to Lucy's request for an interview with the departmental director. He was about to phone through when Lucy asked him to wait while she scrawled a note in Polish for Mr. Mazur. She signed her name Mary Kaminska. The secretary carried the scrap of paper to an inner office while Lucy waited on a handsome, un-upholstered visitor's chair. Presently the boy with the yachtsman's tan returned with the news that Mr. Mazur would see Miss Kaminska in three quarters of an hour. Meanwhile, he suggested she visit the observatory platform at the top of the building and take in the view.

Lucy preferred to sit tight. She scanned the back issues of *Public Voice* left on the table next to her, trying to gauge the subjects of Mazur's opinion polls. It encouraged her to see that while the magazine bulged with reports on Americans' taste in tobacco and toothpaste, political surveys did have their place. The longer she sat on the varnished chair seat, however, the more she found herself fidgeting and squirming. The heat of the day had penetrated the windowless waiting area. Lucy shared the space with no one but the secretary at his desk, and yet she began to fear being found here. She tensed whenever the telephone rang or the door opened. Invariably, it would be a delivery boy rushing in to drop an envelope on the secretary's desk. Invariably, he would leave without so much as a glance in Lucy's direction. Still, she wondered if Mr. Robak had since his arrest mentioned her or her plans. By the end of half an hour, she was watching the clock on the wall, counting the minutes till the promised interview.

At minute thirty-six, the secretary's phone rang. He kept his voice low, but he was looking at Lucy. She feared the worst. When he hung up, he surprised her by speaking in Polish, halting but warmly courteous. He said his name was Tomasz. Tomasz was very sorry, but the director had to attend an emergency meeting with the publisher. Still, Mr. Mazur would look forward to meeting Miss Kaminska at one o'clock, just over an hour from now. Now, Tomasz insisted, she positively had to use the interval to visit the observatory. He told her how to do it. She was to return to the main floor, buy a ticket for fifty cents, then take an express elevator to the fiftieth floor, where she would find postcards, souvenirs, and ice cream stands. That ride would take less than two minutes. Then she would transfer to a shuttle elevator to get up the last four floors to the open-air platform. She'd be at the top of the tallest building in the world with Manhattan's other skyscrapers at her feet.

The boy's new-world enthusiasm infected Lucy, who had had more than enough of her hard chair and fraying nerves. She asked if Tomasz would show her the way. Gee, that would be swell — but it couldn't be done. He had to stay at his post. But Miss Kaminska must go, then come and tell him what she thought.

She knew she must *not* go; sightseeing was no part of her plan. Where had a yen for recreation got her in London? She knew she was too distractible.

She went.

At the ground-floor ticket booth, she almost changed her mind. Between her and the wicket were half a dozen men in navy blue blouses and bell-bottoms jostling and ragging one another in a language she didn't understand. But as she was turning away, one of the sailors caught her hand and thrust a ticket into it with a mumbled *por favor*. The ribbon on his hat read ARA *Moreno*.

"Spain?" she asked.

"Argentina," came the unmumbled reply. Lucy smiled to show that was fine with her.

There was another bunch-up in front of the express elevator; this time, however, the sailors held back to make space for her to board. Then they and a few miscellaneous sightseers filled up the car. They wanted to repeat the gallantry when it was time to transfer to the shuttle elevator for the ascent of the narrowest part of the tower, but Lucy took the winding stairs instead, as did a man in a grey suit. She could hear him puffing as he plodded upwards a half-flight, then a full flight behind her.

The stairs were narrow at the top. There was barely room for them and the elevator in the closed pavilion that sat in the middle of the open-air observatory platform. Emerging, Lucy gratefully felt the sea air on her face and rushed to the chest-high railing. Out there beyond the office towers of Manhattan lay other islands, including the one on which the Statue of Liberty stood, and farther out still the Narrows and the watery road home to Europe. The long view was stirring, but dare she look down? While she didn't think she was afraid of heights, she'd never tested herself at 750 feet above street level. Looking down, she found it was not a straight drop. The square tower, half the height of the building, narrowed in tiers as it ascended, then tapered the last few storeys to the observatory and on up to a spire above it. Below the outside of the railing, a green metal roof punctuated with dormers sloped down several floors to another balcony.

The Argentine sailors had clustered around the north side of the observatory, voicing trumpet, drum, and double bass imitations in evident anticipation of hearing some Harlem jazz that evening. Lucy had thought she was as alone as the limited space would permit, when she abruptly felt someone standing too close behind her. As she wheeled about to her left, she felt something prick her left thigh. The grey little man that had puffed up the stairs behind her was pressing a syringe into her through her skirt, his thumb poised on the plunger.

She drove a fisted right hand into his chest, her only thought to drive him back enough to remove the needle from her leg. He recoiled as intended, only to lunge at Lucy again with his syringe. She dodged right and crouched in one movement. Dropping her handbag, she grabbed the man's ankles as he collided with the railing. She pulled and lifted. With a grunt, over he went — disappearing from Lucy's view down the slope of the roof. She didn't stop to look over the railing, but bolted down the stairs. Nor did she stop on the fiftieth floor to catch the express elevator to street level; she pounded on down another ten floors to where the tower reached its full width. Here she judged there were enough offices that she could wait for an elevator without attracting attention. She switched between elevator and stairs three times more, arriving at last in the lobby and slipping out unnoticed onto Broadway. She was about to hail a cab when she realized she'd left her purse in the observatory.

I stopped Lucy there. Seated on the bed, she was leaning sideways against the headboard with her legs folded under her. She looked comfortable with her tall tower story, unsurprised that these improbable events had occurred. I wasn't there yet. I got up from my chair and began pacing across the room like a barrister in front of the witness box — except that my apartment was only twelve feet wide, and I didn't get to pace far before turning around. Still, it helped me formulate my questions.

She admitted it had been a huge blunder to leave Mazur's reception area, and for such a frivolous purpose. There was no excuse, and the only words of explanation she could offer were, firstly, that she had found the urgings of the sun-kissed Polish-American boy irresistible and, secondly, that she fully believed she hadn't been followed to the Woolworth Building. The grey man had been the best tracker she'd ever dealt with.

He was, I said, clearly a better tracker than a scrapper. Still, I found it hard to believe that a five-foot-five woman could tumble a grown man over a chest-high railing. If that was my problem, Lucy informed me, there were a few things I should bear in mind. The grey man was older and not particularly fit. He had not recovered from his four-storey climb when he approached her. His reactions were slow, his intentions telegraphed. His appreciation of threats

— getting punched in the chest, for example — was dulled. In this context his weapon, the hypodermic needle, became an encumbrance. With none of the slashing capacity of a knife, it was too easy to dodge.

I let that sit for the moment and got Lucy to account for how she got out of the building without interference: it wasn't as if she and the jabber had that crow's nest all to themselves. True, she replied. But the Argentines were caught up in their own affairs by the time she and the grey man reached the platform. The tussle had been brief and quiet. By the time Lucy fled, no one might have noticed that she'd arrived. And if any one of the sailors had witnessed what happened, would his first impulse have been to chase her or to see if the man overboard could be rescued? No one knew if she had a gun. And foreigners might be particularly reluctant to take on police work. I suggested they still might have raised an alarm. They hadn't, though. At least, not in time to stop her, according to Lucy. She doubted any of the men from ARA *Moreno* had enough English to make a coherent report of what had happened, and there would have been no one to report to until the shuttle elevator's next arrival. The operator might have a phone in his car, but Lucy had seen none on the observatory level.

I took four paces from the corridor door to the window over the alley, then four paces more back to the door.

Finally, I asked what Lucy thought had been in the syringe and what had become of it. She didn't know the answer to either question. She thought if the heavens were just, the grey man should have accidentally injected the contents into himself when he fell.

As she ran from the front of the building, Lucy didn't look up to see if the grey man were stuck somewhere on the south face of the tower's steepled roof. She kept her eyes at street level, searching for somewhere private enough to make a withdrawal from the emergency supply of cash in her girdle. The WC of a Chinese restaurant filled the bill. The smell of frying pork and garlic made her mouth water, but she hadn't time to eat. She had already missed the day train to Montreal; if she snagged a cab right away, she could just make the overnight to Toronto.

As Lucy and I now knew, there had been a second tail waiting for her at Grand Central — a second, younger grey man, who had followed her to the Beaconsfield Hotel and engaged in a deadly game of catch with her four mornings ago. On the train, however, he made no move to harm her. He was perhaps awaiting orders; possibly he had no weapon until he made contact with Soviet sympathizers in Toronto. For her part, Lucy struck up an acquaintance during the twenty-hour journey with a tiny spinster in her late sixties, just returning home to Stratford, Ontario, from a week of art galleries in New York. She seemed to Lucy just the person to recommend an inexpensive Toronto hotel where a woman alone might feel safe.

Chapter 12

LIGHT WAS SPILLING INTO my apartment around and between the curtains. It was a cooler morning, though still well above average for September. Lucy made us tea and under protest ate a mess of corn-flakes and condensed milk, pronouncing them a poor breakfast even by Moscow standards.

By now I thought I had the whole of Lucy's story. I couldn't vouch for the truth of every detail, but the stakes were high enough that I had to pass her claims up to where they could be assessed and acted on.

"I want you to come with me to police head-quarters this morning," I said when she'd shoved her cereal bowl aside.

"Will they arrest me, Sergeant?"

"Not if I get my way. What time on Thursday did you check into the Beaconsfield Hotel?"

"Eleven in the morning. I went straight from the station."

I didn't say anything to that.

"Then, after I have hotel room, I went shopping and bought two dresses that didn't make me look like Edna. Do you believe me about Lipetsk?"

"Fritzi's flying school, you mean? The test pilots, the warplanes?" I thought back to Lucy's asking whether I thought Germans surrendered easily, and then back further to those pretty, unscarred German villages on the march from the Belgian border to the Rhine. "Yeah, I buy it — enough of it."

Her grey eyes studied me. "I trust you — I think."

"Don't go overboard. Why me, Lucy? Why did you come to me with your story anyway?"

"How you touched me after the grenade exploded. Not gentle. Gentle I do not trust. But caring, like you wanted the best."

"Recipe for disaster," I said. "We're going to put that padding back on you for the trip in."

She let herself be strapped into the bulletproof vest for the streetcar ride to City Hall. I introduced her to Sanderson, then parked her in an interview room while I sparred with the old coot.

"You didn't report back last night, Paul. Even after I had a constable sent out to your apartment."

"Inspector, I worked Dominion Day in July and the Civic Holiday in August. The duty roster posted last week gave me Labour Day off."

"Notwithstanding —"

"Notwithstanding, I did manage yesterday to prevent an attempted murder in my apartment basement and to apprehend the perpetrator. And to file a full typed report — which I am now, but was not last night, in a position to supplement."

I dove straight into my updated story, one that attributed as little criminality to Lucja Grudzinska as possible. I saw no homicide charge arising from her having thrown the grenade back to John Doe's side of the door. She'd had no other way in that confined hotel room of saving herself, whereas Doe could have run away down the hall and lived. What I impressed upon Sanderson was that Lucy was a Soviet defector with evidence that Russia was helping Germany to rearm illegally. To silence her, the Soviets had made two attempts on her life since her arrival in Toronto. We had to find their next assassin before he struck. That's where I wanted Detective Sergeant Knight and Acting Detective Cruickshank to concentrate their efforts.

"Whoa, Paul." Sanderson had his pipe going by now. "All the international cloak and dagger stuff makes this a case for the Mounted Police, not us. Besides, Knight's off sick with pneumonia. He's only two months shy of retirement, so I doubt that he'll be back. I'll get RCMP Inspector Lachapelle to send someone round to take the woman off our hands."

Sanderson put the receiver from his stick phone to his ear and started dialing.

"Just a minute, sir." I couldn't stomach the idea of handing her over to men that might not care enough about her claims or her safety. Reaching across Sanderson's desk, I pressed the switch hook down before he could complete the call. "Miss Grudzinska isn't a criminal. She doesn't need to be confined; she needs to be protected."

"She would appear to incite violence." Sanderson looked pointedly at the hand that had disabled his phone, then added, "Two assassination attempts in one long weekend."

"Not her fault," I said.

"What's she doing in town anyway?"

"Running for her life."

"Did she enter the country legally?"

"She was desperate."

"No, in other words. Immigration fraud makes it a case for the federal authorities, Paul."

"Suppose I arrest her for assault on the hospital nurse Daisy Bennett — a crime on our own turf."

"I could still hand her over to Claude Lachapelle. We have other work for you to do."

I was starting to choke on the pipe smoke. "Would you let me have a word with Inspector Lachapelle myself, sir? Keeping Lucy in our care in the meantime. In a cell to herself."

"She'll need a bail hearing if we keep her overnight," said the inspector. "Here, open the door; that cough is filthy. I'll let Claude know to expect you, God help him."

I got Lucy's suitcase out of the evidence locker. I took her everything but the stolen passport and the clothes and makeup she'd used for her Edna disguise. Her green dress was going to be a lot more comfortable and create a better impression on the guards than the shirt and slacks of mine she'd been wearing.

When I opened the door to the interview room, Lucy turned from the view of the pigeons in City Hall's courtyard. The bulletproof vest lay on the battered and wobbly wooden table.

"I didn't get my way," I announced. "At least you'll have your own clothes in the lockup."

She had nothing to say to that. She met my eyes with folded arms, still in front of the window. Her back was a dandy target for a sniper, I couldn't help thinking.

"Jail's as safe a place as any for you at the moment. Now we've got to make some prints to replace the ones you gave away in London. Let me have the negatives."

"Someone asked me once before. Good thing I didn't give them to him."

"I'm different."

"Not enough."

"Did Harry North ever save your life?"

"Did *you*, or was it possibly a trick?"

"That was no trick knife I used on the gunman, Lucy. I can show it to you. His blood is on the blade."

Lucy shrugged. Likely she was thinking that an OGPU agent would be capable of hiring someone to stage an assassination attempt and then killing him. She hadn't seen how Ewart died.

"Suit yourself," I said. I wasn't going to prove what a true friend I was by prying the film out of her mouth. "Promise me at least not to break out, not till I see you again?"

"Of course — a Versailles promise, good until I change my mind. And what do you do while I stay in jail?"

"It would be easier if I had the documents to show them, but I'm going to see the Royal Canadian Mounted Police. That's our version of Scotland Yard's Special Branch."

"Who will put you in power — in *the* power of some cute Russian spy."

"Well, they say one swallow doesn't make a summer. The more vamps the better."

I left her to puzzle that one out while I put in a quick call to the Beaconsfield. When Frank Gabor picked up, I asked if he had been on the desk last Thursday at eleven a.m.

"Thursday?"

"The day before Friday — the day before the explosion."

"Sure, Sergeant ... Thursday? No, I'm mistaken. Thursday morning I was sick. The night clerk had to cover for me till noon."

"And Alex Horvath won't tell me any different?"

"No, no. I asked Alex to keep mum, but he'll level with you if you tell him I said it's all right. We don't want to hide anything from the police. Thursday morning I didn't feel good at all."

"Sorry to hear it," I said, actually pleased as punch to get Lucy's story squared with that of the clerks. "It's the sickly sweet schnapps you put away, Frank. Straight whisky makes the mornings easier to take."

On my way to see Lachapelle, I dropped by the Reference Library on College Street to read last Thursday's New York papers. Enough strange things happened every day in that burg that there wasn't room for them all on the front page, but sure enough buried somewhere in each was the tale of the gent that had had to be hauled off a dormer window on the spire of the Woolworth tower. Sprains, strains, and lacerations apart, he wasn't hurt. He claimed to have climbed over the railing on his own. At the time of his rescue, a syringe full of strychnine had been found on the observatory platform, but he denied any knowledge of that. He wouldn't give his name or place of employment and was being sent to Bellevue Hospital for a sanity check. New York police sergeant Dennis Mullaney was identified as the source of information. I looked over Friday's papers too. By then, the scribes had Lucy's grey man pegged as Manfred Krasny, a private detective with the Continental Agency, where his reputation as a tail was unsurpassed. The inference drawn was that he'd let his reviews go to his head and now thought he could follow birds.

No laughter of mine broke the hush of the reading room. I was thinking of the exhausting spasms characteristic of strychnine poisoning — fatally exhausting if paralysis didn't asphyxiate you first. Lucy had dealt gently with Krasny under the circumstances.

Clearly Krasny's opinion of what should be done to her didn't include criminal prosecution, and Krasny was the only one in a position to testify against her. One paper did mention an Argentine sailor's having spotted a woman in Krasny's vicinity just before he went over, but no useful description could be got out of the lad, even with the aid of a Spanish interpreter.

There was no mention of Lucy's dropped handbag. Either it had gone over the edge or had been picked up by someone not willing to come forward.

Outside the library, I caught a streetcar headed towards Yonge Street. A sign under the window said *KEEP ARM IN*, so I stuck my face out instead to catch a bit of a breeze. After a cooler start, the day was heating up to where we'd been all week.

Many Torontonians, including Toronto cops, would have told you there were no Mounties in town. Where would they have stabled their mounts? And what work would there have been for them, after all, when we had our own municipal force, not to mention the Ontario Provincial Police? I don't say the RCMP encouraged such ignorance, but I'm betting it suited them. Much of their work was undercover surveillance of illegal or suspicious organizations. For that, they didn't need horses or publicity. The nineteen men of Western Ontario divisional HQ were, Sanderson had informed me, tucked into the top floor of Postal Station F. When I left the northbound Yonge car at Charles Street, I could see no stable attached — and when I looked up from the sidewalk, I saw no sign touting Canada's official spycatchers in any of the third floor windows.

The building was grand enough with its pillars and balustrades and two shades of stone, still distinguishable under the soot of the twenty years since its construction. All the same, on climbing the two flights of stairs, I found the attic level just as stifling as my own low-rent apartment. A perspiring constable waylaid me at the head of the stairs and led me to Inspector

Lachapelle, who was sipping from a tall glass of water in the southwest corner office and carefully not letting the condensation drip onto the papers spread on the desk in front of him.

The inspector shoehorned me into his schedule just before he went to lunch. A slender greyhound of a man, he looked as if he could use a bite. I wouldn't know an expensive suit if I saw one, but Lachapelle's was well-fitted, well-pressed, and well-brushed and gave this French-Canadian a Savile Row look. His neat moustache was white, his skin pale and unweathered, though not young-looking for his rank. His brown eyes impressed me as alert and impatient. I was dealing with the modern, urban, indoor Mountie.

"Well, Shenstone, was there something your inspector couldn't deal with by telephone?" he said when we were both seated.

"It's a situation our department's not used to," I said. "A woman has turned up with information that could shake up the whole continent of Europe. Specifically make the League of Nations change its mind about admitting Germany tomorrow."

The inspector didn't react to the drama of my announcement. "You'd better pass it on then to the Department of External Affairs in Ottawa, or maybe to the British Foreign Office."

"Time is short, sir. I haven't read the manuals of protocol, but it seems to me the RCMP Security Service would have a better chance of catching Prime Minister King's ear in a hurry than a municipal cop."

"What is this revelation?" the inspector asked.

"Germany's building up an illegal air force. Can you direct me to someone in your outfit that would be of interest to?"

Lachapelle stroked his moustache. "You fight in the last war, Shenstone?"

"Start to finish," I said. "48th Highlanders."

"Royal Corps of Engineers myself."

That explained why the few pictures on his office walls were of bridges. The office was larger than Sanderson's, but spartan, with little distracting clutter. It looked as if its occupant liked to deal with one thing at a time.

"Served in South Africa," the inspector went on. "A bit old for your show, so I never had to deal with the Germans. You went toe to toe with them for four years, and I wonder if you aren't carrying a grudge. I don't see Germans causing trouble these days."

"They're the ones with the grudge, sir. They didn't realize they were beaten in 1918, so they're preparing the next round. In Russia, I might add, to escape the notice of Allied weapons inspectors."

"Ah! Russians are a different matter." The Mountie looked at me with new interest. "Is this woman you mention a Russian Communist?"

"Polish and not a Communist."

"But she lived in Russia after the Revolution?"

"After and before."

"Did she enter Canada legally?"

"No, sir. But she entered Canada to escape Russian Communist assassins. She didn't come to stir up the masses, and she doesn't intend to stay."

Lachapelle opened a folder on his desk and shut it again with a scowl. "My problem right now is that a number of unions are trying to form some Frankenstein monster called the All-Canadian Congress of Labour. She didn't come to help with that, did she?"

"No, sir."

"It's bad enough having the Canadian Brotherhood of Railway Employees involved. They could bring this whole country to a stop."

Lachapelle paused, but I failed to show the consternation he was looking for. I was thinking of Beaconsfield guest Floyd Peters, young husband and railway union activist.

"Then," said the inspector, "there's the Mine Workers of Canada — a union run by Communists and making no bones about it."

"She's nothing to do with either of those."

At this point, the overheated constable came by with a Thermos of ice water to refill the inspector's glass. In his tightly buttoned tunic, he looked as if he could have used a drink himself; I wondered if I'd live long enough to see Mounties form a union. The Toronto Police had had one, which the men on top had busted up while I was overseas.

I picked up the thread with Lachapelle. "I understand that you're worried about the spread of the Communist philosophy to Canadian workers. The case I came to speak to you about involves a new and different threat from Russia. Two threats, in fact. First, good old-fashioned militarism in concert with a remilitarized Germany. Second, the employment

of Communist Party of Canada members to liqui-
date a defector that would alert the West to threat
number one."

"Are you saying, Shenstone, that there is no danger of Bolshevist revolution in this country?"

In fact, I never had lost sleep worrying over home-
grown Bolshevist revolution — not because I thought
it harmless, rather because I thought it impossible.
I'd never been able to root out the conviction that too
many of us since pioneer days have wanted to plough
our own furrow and make our own voices heard on
election day. That's why I'd never got my tail in a knot
about the Communist Party of Canada. The last three
days had admittedly changed me. I now feared the
CPC, but only insofar as Russia was using it to recruit
assassins for non-Marxist ends.

Nevertheless, to keep things sweet with Lachapelle,
I was willing to play the agnostic regarding the violent
overthrow of capitalism.

"No, sir, I'm not saying that. The line the Soviets
push today is that they're keeping socialism inside
their own borders, for themselves alone. How sincere
they are would be for you to assess."

"Not your field — correct? Well, a military buildup
overseas is not my field. Was there anything else?"

"Yes, Inspector." I took Edna Salisbury's passport
from my jacket pocket. "I can see you're busy. I'm
sorry if you can't get your service to take Germany's
rearmament seriously. But I'd ask you not to waste
your valuable time prosecuting the messenger. Here is
the Commonwealth of Australia passport she travelled

on. I'm giving it to you so the issuer may be notified, and so you know that no further fraudulent use will be made of it."

The inspector had been sitting at attention since mention of the word *Russian*.

"All right," he said at last, visibly relaxing, "so long as I don't hear the woman has been attending union meetings or giving speeches."

"There's something else I'd like to ask you," I went on. "I'm concerned about the potential for violence within the CPC. The last attempt to murder Lucja Grudzinska was made by a gunman named Dan Ewart, who committed suicide to avoid being questioned. How many more men of that kidney are we to expect?"

"Sergeant, I believe any member of the Communist Party capable of the vilest crimes. If we learn that any of these rascals is contemplating violence, we shall stop him in his tracks."

"Can I assume then that you had no advance warning of the danger Ewart posed?"

"Personally, I had none."

"And you have no idea who is most likely to be the next Dan Ewart?"

Lachapelle raised his arms and lowered them. "I have nothing to tell you at the moment."

"Let's hope a later moment won't be too late. The Toronto attacks on Miss Grudzinska were made by Mills bomb and by revolver. Can you tell me if these weapons are acquired as the occasion demands or if the party is keeping a cache that could be seized?"

My question sparked a fleeting, startled look before the inspector got his mask of protocol back in place. "Information requests of the kind you're making would have to come from further up the chain of command," he said. "Would your chief constable be willing to call my superintendent?"

"Yes, sir." A bold lie was what was wanted and what I gave him, though I hoped to make it true soon enough.

"Very well, Shenstone. Then I may be able to do something for you." He dropped Edna's passport into a drawer with no more than a glance.

I thought the conversation was over and was getting up to leave when I caught a look of irritation cross Lachapelle's face. For the briefest moment, his mouth muscles tightened and a blood vessel stood out on his lean neck. I paused to see if he had more to say.

He did, and when he spoke, his tone was unexpectedly confiding. "It might surprise you as a detective sergeant to learn how little discretion an inspector has, how little influence — however well educated he may be. At the same time, those pilots whose stunts we read about in the newspapers every week can go anywhere and be listened to, even if they never graduated from grade twelve. Look at that Whitehead fellow — on a first-name basis with the whole federal cabinet, acquainted with the Prince of Wales. People make a fuss over him as if he'd won the war. Not really his fault, I suppose: he's a perfectly sound and decent chap."

"Is he, sir?" I asked, startled by how very English Lachapelle sounded. I could imagine he might like to chum around with royalty himself.

"Straight as a string, no political involvement whatever — I've checked. But you were on the ground, Shenstone. You know where the war was won. If I were you, I wouldn't worry about a German air force. Airplanes will never be more than a sideshow, even if the daredevils that ride in them do get the attention."

By the time I got out of the RCMP offices, I'd revised my estimate of Lachapelle's age upwards by about twenty years. But I had got one unlooked-for benefit from our meeting: the idea that flyers had influence and that Kip Whitehead knew the heir to the throne. Who better to warn of a resurrected German air force than an air force expert like Kip? He'd understand that the next air war would be no sideshow — nor a joust of pilot officers, chivalrously saving each other from frostbite. It would be a war of death from the air, waged against soldiers and civilians alike with a thoroughness beyond old men's imagining.

Before we could get to work on Whitehead, I had to spring Lucy. And before I could do that, I had a phone call to make. I made it from Uneeda Lunch on Queen Street, talking around a cheese sandwich — quite a chunk of which I got down while waiting for the folks at Toronto Western Hospital to figure out that Daisy Bennett had come off duty at eight a.m. and was likely sleeping off the effects of an overnight shift. By chance, it was Jane Sparrow that picked up the phone at the nurses' residence. She remembered me all right, but that didn't make her eager to oblige me at the cost of disturbing her friend's rest. I said the matter was urgent and confidential. I repeated myself

until I wore her down, and by the time I'd drunk a
cup of coffee a drowsy voice was announcing that the
speaker on the line was D. Bennett. She didn't exact
apologies for being woken, and I got to the point.

"Miss Bennett, have you suffered any ill effects
from the attack on you last Friday?"

"A little notoriety in the residence." She turned
away from the mouthpiece to yawn and came back
with a brisker voice. "Fully recovered otherwise."

"Glad to hear it," I said.

"I did have to pay for new glasses and a new
uniform."

"Just what I was thinking. Now if you were to
receive full financial compensation for losses arising
out of that attack, would you consider the affair ade-
quately dealt with?"

"What do you mean, Sergeant?"

"Lucy Clarkson was admitted to Toronto Western
Hospital because of a blow to the head. That blow *may*
have diminished her criminal responsibility. Hard to
say since no doctor ever saw her, but — practically
speaking — it might be hard to get her convicted for
what she did to you."

"I see. You were afraid I might be clamouring for
a pound of her flesh."

"Set me straight."

"That's not the way the medical world works —
not my little corner of it. We're protective of patients,
even difficult ones, and not really in the business of
punishing. Besides, I'm inclined to put the blame
elsewhere. If the hospital had been told that Miss

Clarkson had been involved in a crime, we might have been more watchful."

"So you won't object if charges against her are dropped?"

"She's been apprehended?"

"Yes."

"No, I won't object."

"And you'll accept the offer of compensation?"

"Was the money in her undergarment hers?"

"She won it in a legal game of cards."

"Then she's better off than I am. Financially, at least. I'd like to hear her story sometime when I don't crave sleep quite so much."

We left it there, and I returned to HQ thinking Daisy Bennett was a pretty good egg after all. Of course, it didn't take much to make me like a woman.

When I reached my desk, I found Ned Cruickshank seated there drinking a glass of milk and shaking his head over my report on the Dan Ewart scrap.

"I'm wondering now if there might have been anything in Ewart's war record to suggest a blood-thirsty streak. Clearly, Sergeant, I didn't check into this character as thoroughly as I ought."

"You can make up for it now. Find out where he got the gun, where he got the cyanide, where he got his training, and who else has them. If I can get Inspector Sanderson to put the request through the proper channels, you should get some help from the RCMP."

"There are no RCMP in Toronto, are there?"

"I was talking to one of their inspectors less than an hour ago. But if the chief constable is of your opinion, we may not see Mounties speeding to our rescue anytime soon. Start without them."

"But where do they —"

I told Ned to forget about the horses. Then I briefed him on Manfred Krasny's attempt on Lucy's life and asked him to draft a telegram to a New York cop named Dennis Mullaney.

"Let's see if Mullaney can tell us anything about our John Doe. We believe Krasny and Doe followed Lucy from Chelsea Piers to Grand Central Terminal. There they split up, with Krasny tailing her to the Woolworth Building and Doe waiting at the station to see if she'd use either of the train tickets she'd bought. When she boarded the overnight to Toronto, Doe followed her. Oh, and, Ned — mail Mullaney a photo of Doe's remains. The grenade didn't leave much of his face. Still, something there might trigger a memory."

"The attempts are quite different, aren't they, Sergeant?" Ned commented. "I mean, Doe and Krasny both seemed clumsy — not at surveillance, but when it came to killing. Ewart appears to have been tougher. More professional, even in his choice of weapons."

"Good point — and if Lucy hadn't been wearing a bulletproof vest, he would have succeeded."

It occurred to me that, while they had no trouble recruiting informers abroad through the various countries' Communist parties, assassinations on foreign soil were something new for the Russians. Unluckily, they were learning fast. German agents would have been more efficient. But, unless the Weimar Republic had their own Harry North in MI5, the Germans still mightn't know that their rearmament secret was out. Moscow wouldn't be bragging to Berlin about Lucy's visit to Lipetsk and subsequent disappearance.

I hadn't time to give Ned the full story now. He'd have to pick it up as he went along. "Know what you're doing?" I asked him. "Don't be shy about getting the constables to give you a hand. One more thing, Ned: I need someone that can translate Russian into English. Someone reliable."

Sanderson couldn't see me just then, so I wrote him a memo regarding my interview with Lachapelle and my concern about a secret cache of weapons. I asked the office stenographer Eric Lindstrom to find out the fastest way to contact Wing Commander Christopher Whitehead of the RCAF. Then I did the paperwork necessary for Lucy's release. As no charges against her were going to be pursued, either by our department or by the Mounties, she was no longer under arrest.

If the news pleased her, she didn't let it show. I found her icy calm, and at the same time suspicious of me, as I guess she'd a right to be. I explained about laying her case before Kip Whitehead and the need to obtain prints and translations of her documents first. We had no facilities at City Hall to process film; the department always sent it down the block to Abbot and Stuart Quick Finish Photo, so that's where we went too. Lucy insisted on standing in their darkroom all the time her negatives were in use.

On the other hand, she raised no objection when I mentioned using a portion of her three hundred dollars to square her debts.

"Of course. You pay and bring me what remains."

"There'll be lots left," I assured her. "Fifteen bucks should re-outfit the nurse you choked and robbed. How much was the raincoat?"

"For the coat and hat, ten dollars."

"Which shop?"

"La something — La Vogue. Give the nurse thirty: I scared her a lot."

On my way out, I thumbed through the photo shop's phone directory and found a Dundas West address for La Vogue Ladies Wear — just over a mile from the Western Hospital.

I left Lucy at Abbot and Stuart while I crossed the street to the Dominion Bank. A teller familiar with the scale of my usual transactions tried not to look surprised upon receiving three of Uncle Sam's C-notes. After deducting a service charge, he handed me back almost as much in Canadian funds. I deposited forty dollars in my own account, then wrote cheques in the amounts Lucy specified to the clothing store and to Daisy Bennett. By the time I'd mailed these, Lucy was waiting for me at the photo shop with the prints. And back at City Hall, Ned had located a professor of Russian literature at the university.

Lucy frowned and clicked her tongue; she didn't see why her own translation of the documents shouldn't be good enough. I pointed out that she had no Canadian credentials or references — and that, while her Russian might be impeccable, her English was still hit and miss.

"What is *impec* — oh, very smart! But I will bet you all I have that your university professor does not use that word even once in his translation."

"I can't match all you have," I said truthfully, having just looked at my bank balance. "And you'd better hang on to your cash. Anything you could do to make that much in short order is illegal in this town, gambling included."

"And then you'd have to arrest me all over again. Always the good cop!"

"Not quite. They're not paying me to report on German war preparations. So, if my inspector asks, this meeting with Professor Snodgrass was to get a lead on who gave the assassin in my apartment basement his orders."

Chapter 13

AS IT TURNED OUT, I missed meeting Professor Snodgrass by the narrowest of margins. Lucy and I were heading out the door when my phone called me back. I answered standing up.

"Paul, I have something for you." An accented voice, not loud but portentous.

"Your name, sir?" I was preparing to hand him over to Detective Sergeant Crate, who sat reading *Punch* magazine at the desk three to the right of mine.

"It's Willy."

"Go on." There were thousands of Willies in town; it was lowering to be suspected of knowing only one — but then it came to me. "Stinson?"

"I thought you'd remember me."

Remembering Willy Stinson, born Constantinov, a typesetter at the *Examiner*, gave me no pleasure. Four years back, around the time I was first promoted to the Detective Department, Stinson's wife and her lover were killed with two .32 calibre bullets apiece, and Willy was reported to be telling friends the hand of justice had been his own. The investigation, in which I'd played a subordinate rôle, had been rushed, the prosecution undertaken before the murder weapon had been found. No witness admitted to having heard a confession. The jury acquitted. The detective in charge held a grudge against Stinson, kept an eye out for any excuse to punish him. Then finally — months later — the detective waltzed into the office one afternoon rubbing his hands. Stinson's name had been found on a Communist Party of Canada list of new members. Party membership was a criminal code offence punishable by up to twenty years in prison, but I argued that no punishment inflicted on Stinson for his politics could square the accounts of the man and woman we all believed the typesetter had slain. Inspector Sanderson settled the matter. He discovered from the RCMP Security Service that it was Commissioner Starnes's policy not to create political martyrs by charging individuals for CPC membership unless other seditious acts were involved. To my embarrassment, word had got back to Stinson that I had opposed his arrest. I even got a damned thank-you note.

"What is it, Willy? Make it snappy: I'm on my way out."

"It's about Dan Ewart."

That's when my plans changed.

"Hold on." I called to Ned, who was talking on Knight's line. I told him to take Lucy and her prints to the professor's and bring her straight back to HQ.

He nodded, and I watched the two of them leave. They looked like teacher and schoolboy if not quite mother and son. I wondered if Ned would be able to protect her from an attack or to hold her if Lucy took a notion to fly the coop again. But I had to find out what Stinson had. "Okay, Willy. What about Ewart?"

"I read about him in this morning's paper. He tried to kill a woman and committed suicide, right?"

"What about it?"

"You were there, right? It's your case."

"A+ for literacy! What have you got?"

"A letter from Ewart."

"To you?"

"To me, to be opened if he were arrested or if he died."

My scalp tingled. "You were that close to him, Willy?"

"Not really. I got to get rid of this letter, Paul. The Mounties want to talk to me about the strike. They have my apartment staked out. I can't afford to be caught with this. Do you want it or do I burn it?"

"Can you bring it here?"

"The police station?"

He didn't need to say more. "Eaton's cafeteria then — in five minutes."

"Fifteen."

Eaton's department store lay just east of City Hall on the north side of Queen Street. The basement cafeteria was clean and bright with easy-to-clean Formica surfaces everywhere and no dingy alcoves for a tail to hide in. I took my coffee to a corner table. While

I waited I ran through what Dan Ewart and Willy Stinson might have in common: both Communists, both typesetters (even if Ewart hadn't recently been working as such and Stinson was on strike), both capable of shooting people dead — unless, of course, Stinson were innocent of those two murders he'd been charged with as well as "not guilty."

After ten minutes Stinson appeared in the doorway wearing blue denim overalls and a white shirt buttoned to the neck. He paused a moment, then made straight for my table. There was nothing conspicuous about the way he moved, nothing either furtive or swaggering. His appearance too was ordinary. He was thin, of average height, not bad looking. Sadder, I judged, than at the time of his trial, with pouchy eyes and white showing under the irises. His black hair was on the short side and without a part. His short, thick moustache put me in mind of Charlie Chaplin on a cold day in the Klondike. He sat beside me so he could see the room. If on the phone he'd sounded hesitant, he was all dispatch now.

He placed before me a thin envelope torn open at one end and inscribed as Stinson had said: "Open in case of my death or arrest." The narrow-nib handwriting on the envelope and on the single sheet I removed from it recalled the writing I had glimpsed on the papers in Ewart's room at the Beaconsfield: carefully formed, unsloping letters — without curlicue flourishes, but distinguished by long, straight T-crossings.

"When did Dan give you this?" I asked.

"Saturday night. He said he was on his way to a restaurant where Polish people gather, but he wasn't going to feed his face."

"He say anything else — like what he *was* going to do?"

"No, that was it."

The letter in full read:

> *You have already given material help.*
> *Now you must finish the job. You are*
> *the only man that can be trusted to*
> *do it.*
>
> *You would give your life to the*
> *Communist revolution in this country*
> *if the Comintern judged the time right.*
> *You would not flinch from bloodshed.*
> *Now you must be just as zealous in*
> *slaying a traitor to the Soviet Union*
> *and recovering the secrets she stole. She*
> *is known variously as Lucy Clarkson,*
> *Edna Salisbury, and Lucja or Svetlana*
> *Grudzinska. Expect further instruc-*
> *tions from agent Harbinger.*

I tapped my finger on the name. "Who's Harbinger?"

"No idea," Stinson replied.

"Party member?"

"No one I've heard about."

I tucked the letter into its envelope and the envelope into my pocket. "Where are you supposed to find this woman he wants you to kill?"

"I assume she's under your protection."

"Willy, you read about Ewart's death, or you wouldn't have opened this. So you know that the woman Ewart shot at fled the scene and that her present whereabouts are unknown."

"Yeah? Well, not everything is in the newspaper. Especially not that scab version of the *Examiner*."

"I'm surprised you'd even look at it. What material help did you give Ewart?"

Willy avoided my eyes. "I guess I loaned Dan a couple of dollars."

"You guess?"

"Look, I did you a favour by coming here. I thought I owed you something for keeping me out of jail. But now you've got it all, and I'm expected on the picket line. I'm done."

I grabbed his wrist as he made to get up from the table. "Uh-uh, Willy," I said. "You're not done, because sometime soon Harbinger is going to find you and press you hard. You're going to have to decide what you committed yourself to by signing up with the party. Were you volunteering to fight for workers' rights or to butcher a stranger? You might be capable of killing a woman, but not one that never did you wrong."

"Let me go," he growled. "I never killed anyone."

"No, of course not. But when Harbinger gets in touch, I've a hunch you'll be calling me. And it won't be to do me favours." I let him go then, and we both stood up. "Maybe I'll be able to do you one," I said with a dark grin.

It was close to four by the time I got back to HQ. Detective Sergeant Crate was coming out of Sanderson's office, so I slipped in before the inspector got started on something else. After telling him about the meeting with Stinson, I suggested sending a man down to the *Examiner* picket line. If we slapped a tail on Stinson right away, we stood a fair chance of finding out who Harbinger was. Unluckily, Sanderson had just been treated to an earful from the Deputy Chief Constable on the subject of bicycle thefts. It wasn't a matter of the occasional prank: there seemed to be a ring scooping up four or five machines from a respectable neighbourhood in an afternoon, loading them into a van, and selling them in another city. Not incidentally, the grandson of a member of the police commission had lost two new bikes to these bandits, a CCM and a Raleigh. Sanderson had just assigned Rudy Crate to the case, but he wanted me working on it too. I wondered — not aloud — how many detectives it took to tell kiddies to lock their wheels in their parents' garages; aloud I wondered how we were to proceed with investigating the plot against Miss Grudzinska.

"I've said it before, Paul. Hand it to the Mounties. This is right up their alley."

"Inspector Lachapelle is a stickler for proper channels," I ventured. "He wants his superintendent contacted by our chief. I need another couple of days on this assassination business — just so we don't drop the baton between runners."

"Twenty-four hours, Paul, and get to work on the bicycle thing at the same time."

Judging that further argument would only waste what little time I had, I extricated myself from Sanderson's office. Ned and Lucy still weren't back from the university, so I straddled a chair turned backwards in front of Crate's desk. Crate was a tall, stout, pink Englishman, in age somewhere between me and the elderly majority of the thirty detective sergeants. His balding head was bent over the reports of the missing bicycles.

"How many of the owners can provide serial numbers?" I asked.

"You're a scream," Crate observed mirthlessly. "Some can't even tell us the make. Numbers? Not a prayer. They all know the colour, though. Black, black, black, black ... Ah, here's a red one."

"It'll be black by now. How many were locked?"

"More than half — surprised you there!"

"But ..."

"But eight of those only had their wheels immobilized without being chained to anything fixed. Easy targets if you weren't expecting to ride away. And the rest were secured with the keyless padlock."

"Combination locks," I suggested.

"Bless you, Shenstone. Nothing so secure." Crate handed me a padlock from the centre drawer of his desk. The hasp was down and held in the casing, on which no keyhole or dial was to be seen. "Now press firmly just there."

I pressed. The lock sprung open.

"Every Danziger lock responds the same way to pressure at that spot. As even your dim, colonial intellect will grasp, once the secret got out to the criminal element, the lock became useless."

I said we should ask the department to buy some bikes we could inconspicuously mark and leave in tempting locations. Crate said he'd tried this suggestion on Sanderson and been lectured on budget realities.

"You're a well-spoken guy, Rudy," I said. "You might try asking a few prominent gents of the town if they'd fork out fifty dollars apiece to buy decoys. Say the bikes will be distributed to the deserving poor in their names after the thieves are convicted."

"Call any of them a gent and he'd be as likely to draw and quarter you as open his wallet." Crate had once helpfully warned me that it sounded childish to call a ginger snap a cookie; the correct term was *bickie*.

"That's what I mean, Rudy. I wouldn't know what to say: I'd be hopeless at it. I'll leave it to you."

I went to see what Lindstrom had learned about where to find Kip Whitehead. Here luck was with me. The aviator was flying down from Ottawa to Toronto this very afternoon. He was already in the air and was expected at Leaside field around seven thirty, shortly before sunset. Lindstrom didn't know Whitehead's programme for the evening, but I was determined that Lucy and I would wedge ourselves into it.

The thing still nagging at me was not knowing where Harbinger was. I worried that he had followed Lucy when she left City Hall to get the translations — although rationally I didn't see how Harbinger would know what Lucy looked like.

Unless John Doe had taken one on the train, OGPU agents in Toronto likely wouldn't have a photo of her yet. Just one week ago today, Harry North's Marconigram had established that the woman with Edna Salisbury's passport was headed for New York. Lucy's liner took nine days to sail from the U.K. to the U.S., and I hadn't heard of any ship crossing the Atlantic east to west in much under five. There was no way mail could arrive faster. The three attempts on Lucy's life on this continent had presumably all been targeted on the basis of personal identification — a disembarking *Luxuria* passenger had pointed her out to Doe and Krasny; Doe had followed her to the Beaconsfield where Ewart had been able to pick her up. Then Ewart died before he could point her out to anyone else.

Harbinger might well know what *I* looked like: one of the papers this morning had illustrated their coverage of the Ewart business with an old photo of the detective involved. It might then be assumed that any woman I was accompanying was Lucy, but Lucy was with Ned at present, not me. That left only the possibility that my arrival with Lucy in the morning had been observed. I should have sent her on into City Hall ahead of me. And we shouldn't be seen leaving City Hall together this evening.

I phoned the university and got put through to Professor Snodgrass's office. The Russian expert sounded excited and impatient. I asked if Detective Cruickshank was still there, and Ned's voice came on the line. He said they were just wrapping up. Situated as he was, it wouldn't have been diplomatic to tell me what the holdup had been, but I could imagine that Lucy had had her say on Russian aeronautical lingo and that there had been a good deal of back and forth between the spy and the academic.

"Change of plan, Ned," I said. "Don't bring Lucy back to headquarters. I'll meet you — where?" I had a two-birds-one-stone idea. "On the campus there, the chemistry lab, in the basement of the Mining Building. Yes, that's where it is — don't ask it to make sense. College Street at the north end of McCaul. Got it? Half an hour."

From the evidence locker, I retrieved the Smith and Wesson .32 Safety Hammerless that Ewart had fired at Lucy. We already had someone tracing the revolver's history through the serial number, but now I planned to take it to our forensic science brain, Dalton Linacre, for a possible match to the bullets that had killed Gala Stinson and Pierre Vezina in 1922. Just in case what Ewart called *material help* from Willy Stinson turned out to be the loan of something more than a couple of dollars. Linacre was overworked but liked ballistics a whole lot better than bombs and sounded game when I called him up to tell him what I was bringing along.

I left Sanderson a note. He was on the phone so I didn't have to take any static. I slipped out of City Hall through the courtyard and what we cops thought of as the Black Maria gate, although it was used for the delivery of supplies for all the offices in the building. By now rush hour had hit in full force: the streets and the streetcars were full of sources of heat. Only this morning I'd thought that the weather had broken, that cooler September days were at last beginning, but you'd never have guessed it if you could have stood on first the Bay and then the College car, stood propped up by bodies sweating through their cotton coverings or hemming you round with their woollen suits. It was nearing twenty-four hours since my last shuteye, and that handcuffed sleep hadn't rested me much. I nearly slumbered standing up; if any of the wooden seats had been free, I'd have been a goner. Not a good thing for an officer carrying two pistols, one of them loaded.

The wide basement corridor of the Mining Building was cool and welcoming. I trailed a burning hand along the ceramic tiles that lined the lower part of the walls. For the last quarter year I'd been on close enough terms with Professor Linacre to open his door without knocking. The good feeling hadn't resulted from long heart-to-hearts. On the contrary, he appreciated the speed with which I came to the point, and I liked his pointed reports. I'd recently told him it was his fault we didn't have a crime lab in Toronto as they had in Montreal and Los Angeles; the chemistry professor was so good at his forensics sideline that the government didn't see why it should spend money to set up a fully-staffed separate facility. To which he'd replied that the deceased I'd been interested in had been killed not by accidentally contaminated milk but by deliberately poisoned strawberry jam. Linacre was as close to a crime-fighting hero as my work ever brought me. It gave me a lift to see him sitting bent over his microscope in his worn, black suit, his limp, yellowing lab coat, and a flamboyant, hummingbird-green bow tie.

"White tags on the table by the door. Attach one to the gun and write down what you want done with it."

"As I said on the phone —"

"I remember what you said on the phone, but I may not in an hour. Write it down, please." Linacre looked up at me with a grin. "How late will there be someone to take a call at your office?"

I told him Sanderson was usually there till eight, sometimes ten. Linacre said to write eight p.m. on the back of the tag. I followed his instructions and closed the door behind me on my way out.

Lucy's laugh preceded her into the basement hall where it echoed around. I intercepted her and Ned just inside the College Street entrance. When I asked what the joke was, she said she'd tell me later. Her face was shiny with moisture, not surprising in view of the temperature outdoors, but the look unexpectedly became her. I thought of how this woman, grey now beginning to show in her hair, had spent her whole girlhood in grand causes and now faced the re-annihilation of her homeland. A popular song asked the question, "Ain't We Got Fun?" The answer in Lucy's case would have to be *not much yet*.

It was nearing Ned's five o'clock quitting time, but when I explained the deadline Sanderson had imposed on us, he volunteered to tell his mother he wouldn't be home for dinner.

I asked him to go back to HQ to study the arrest photo of Willy Stinson, then down to the *Examiner* picket line. "If Stinson's still there, ask if Harbinger has contacted him yet." I showed Ned Ewart's note to Stinson. "If not, tail Stinson as long as you can."

"You want me to apprehend this Harbinger guy when he makes his move. And if —"

"If anything unexpected comes up, rely on your own initiative."

When Ned had left, I confirmed that Snodgrass's translations jibed with the ones Lucy had done. Then I told her I proposed to place her evidence of clandestine German war preparations before an influential air force officer. We should set out for Leaside airfield about seven.

"And can we trust this officer to not be another Harry North?" Lucy wanted to know.

"I think so — and there's nowhere else we can turn." I was thinking that if Whitehead were rotten, we hadn't really won the war.

"So ... What do we do until seven? Back to your apartment?"

I said I didn't think that would be safe.

Lucy wiped her forehead with the back of her hand. "My hotel then."

"You don't have a hotel."

"You choose one for me."

No better arrangement came to mind. I had to stick with Lucy so long as Harbinger remained unaccounted for. I chose the Gladstone Hotel, across from the Parkdale railway station, on the same run of Queen Street West as the Beaconsfield, but altogether more confidence-inspiring.

On the way out there, we ducked into the Beaconsfield so I could check Dan Ewart's signature in the register against the handwriting of the note Stinson had given me. A fair match — down to the long, arrow-straight crossing of the *t*. I'd have preferred a larger writing sample, but Ewart had checked out before his attack on Lucy, so his notebook wasn't available.

The Gladstone Hotel occupied the northeast corner of Queen and Gladstone, with four-storey façades on both streets. Where they met, a square tower and cupola rose three quarters as high again. Round arches topped off windows and balconies. The style resembled that of City Hall, only in red brick rather than pink and buff stone. The woman at the desk commented on Lucy's lack of luggage, but when I showed her my badge she quieted down and handed over the key to Room 204. The elevator let us out into a rectangular hall big enough for a dance or a game of basketball. Lucy's room was down a corridor on the left side.

I settled into an armchair and suggested Lucy might like to get some rest. Before I knew it she was sitting in my lap with an arm around my neck.

"No handcuffs, Sergeant?"

"Lucy, I don't think this is a good idea."

This now involved her ruffling my hair and playing with my ear.

"I stayed all morning in jail while you ran around. My head is more rested than yours, so I better know what is a good idea."

I lifted her in my arms and deposited her on the bed. Her grey eyes accused me of such unfriendliness that I couldn't plop back into my chair without giving her shoulder a squeeze. She gripped my hand and kissed it. All at once what had not seemed like a good idea seemed like the only idea, or something better than any idea. I knelt by the bed and used my imprisoned hand to raise Lucy's face to mine, her lovely lips to mine.

There was about her love play a frisky innocence I should have found surprising in view of her rough and tumble history. But I was thinking of neither past nor future. There was as much joy in the moment as my body had ever felt, or my eyes had ever seen on a woman's face.

Afterwards, we lay side by side on the bed in the few clothes we hadn't got around to shedding. Lucy propped herself on one elbow and looked down into my face.

"When we kissed," she said, "did you think of my dental plate?"

"Naw — I was too busy thinking of your peg leg."

"My *what?*"

"Never mind. Wake me at seven, will you?"

Chapter 14

THERE WERE CONSEQUENCES, OF course. Lucy woke me at ten to seven with the idea that if we hung my shirt and suit jacket in the shower for ten minutes some of the wrinkles would be less obvious. All very domestic. And she stopped calling me *sergeant*.

"Paul," she said in the back of the taxi, making two syllables of it, *pa-ul*, "could we stop somewhere to buy cigarettes?"

I didn't look at my watch. "We haven't time."

"You don't smoke, do you?"

"I drink. I can't afford more than one vice." I took her hand.

She squeezed mine back. "I thought every soldier smoked."

"Some that were gassed don't."

Our cab was jogging west along Merton Street, just north of Mount Pleasant Cemetery. The sun shone hot and orange horizontally through the dusty rear window, setting fire to Lucy's cheek when she turned to look at me. It was a lovelier face than I'd first thought it, and no easier to read.

"They say the next war will be fought with poison gas sprayed from airplanes."

"Who says, Lucy? Your Commander Trigorin?"

"Stronger poison than anything used in the last war. All the people in a city could be killed and all the buildings left for the invaders to use."

"You don't need to stir me up for this meeting we're going to. I'm in — one hundred percent." I dropped my voice and put my mouth close to her ear. "Is that what the cute stuff in bed was about? Tying me in tighter and closer to make sure I wouldn't let you down when we're up against it?"

We swayed in our seats without speaking as the cab wound its way up McCrae Drive towards the airfield.

"At the university, you asked me why I was laughing with Ned," Lucy said at last.

"Yeah?"

"Twice in two days you called me vamp: I asked Ned what it meant. He turned red, so I tried to make it a joke. Vampire, ha-ha! Vampire, swallow — it's the same. I don't mind. Mostly I use men, yes. But for you it's easier to think I do always. You don't want to believe anyone could like you — just for you."

I thought the psychology lame but sweet. "I like you too, Lucy. But even if I couldn't stand the sight of you, I'd still be dead against this new German air force."

"At Lipetsk, after I found that letter, I felt scared every time I saw or heard warplanes firing up their engines. Soon, I thought, they will be taking off from runways on the Polish-German border. But why should you care? You have never been to my country."

"I've seen what a bully can do to smaller neighbours," I said, "and not just in battle. Towns torched to intimidate the populace, civilians shot. We were too late to prevent all that in Belgium. In Poland, there's still time. Now get ready to do the sales job of your life."

The taxi had stopped at the edge of a grass field. Before us stretched an east-west runway, defined by two rows of what looked like bonfires, laid but not lit. Outside these limits, around the edge of the field, were dotted utilitarian, clapboard buildings — leftovers from a wartime flying school. From a two-storey block of offices on our left hung a banner proclaiming, "Leaside Airport is run by the Toronto Flying Club, for the benefit of the municipality." Of the dozen hangars, many were of the portable timber-and-canvas variety. In front of them stood planes reflecting no recent developments in aeronautical engineering. As far as I could see, all were single-engine, one- or two-seat biplanes made of wood and canvas — either disarmed Great War aircraft or civilian adaptations of the same. There was nothing like the single-wing, all-metal Junkers that had carried Lucy to and from Lipetsk.

Some twenty people could be seen, some working on the machines, more standing or sitting in the grass at the near end of the runway, chatting and smoking and surveying the eastern sky. Their backs were to us, but they looked happy.

Stepping out of the car, we found the wind, like the setting sun, at our backs. The people that had been sitting got to their feet. A girl with red hair was pointing up at something the size of a flea. Then it was the size of a housefly and getting bigger fast. Making straight for us from the east, a single-engine biplane grew as it slid down towards the uneven earth of the airfield. It touched, bounced, and grappled with the ground more determinedly, plowing the runway with its tail skid, shuddering to a stop ten yards in front of us. Two figures in head-to-toe flying suits clambered out and into the welcoming arms of the bystanders, some dressed for flying, more not.

For a confused moment, I thought this couldn't be Kip's plane, for the pilot was less tall and lean than the former ace. It was Beatrice Whitehead, of course, as I saw when she pulled off her tight leather helmet to release billows of blond hair. It was only the second time I'd seen her in person. Her face was full, her complexion youthful and healthy. Her broad smile greeted everyone and she seemed to know everyone's name.

"Hi, Joan. Moe, you're here too — how lovely! Bet you've got my Bristol fuelled up and ready to go. Still waiting for that Renault V12, Larry? Gosh, they must be shipping it by rowboat. Anyone have a cigarette?"

Her accent was no more than a light seasoning to her chatter; in fact, I wouldn't even have identified it as Italian if I hadn't known.

Kip stood watching at her side — a beat or two behind in saying his own hellos.

"How are you, Gus? No, just be here for a couple of hours to tune up and chow down. I want to do some solo night flying. That's why they broke out the boundary lights. Yeah, the busy Bea came down to pick up a Bristol F.2B and fly her back to Ottawa. The trip was her idea actually. Anyway, we'll both be on our own. Good practice, but less fun."

The golden boy looked as if he was used to having fun and — this was the truly winning part — was grateful for it. The dogfights he'd won in the Italian Alps had not made him arrogant or cold. He had three quarters of the looks a man would need to model suits in a glossy magazine ad. For the rest, his fair hair, centre-parted and perpetually overdue at the barber's, combined with his untamed eyebrows to put you in mind of a shaggy pup. He looked no different from when we'd last met.

"Wing Commander!" I called out as I pushed forward. "Still driving that Hispano-Suiza H6?"

I'd first seen it as it pulled away from me out of the back lot of Wyndham's garage on Eastern Avenue. The six-cylinder engine was powerful enough to make it disappear fast, but the driver had only just let in the clutch when I got the barrel of my Webley revolver lined up with my eye and blasted a slug into the right rear tire. The driver, Wyndham himself, decided not to risk becoming the target of a second shot and slammed on the engine-assisted brakes, bringing the H6 to a clean stop half in the lot, half in the road. The dirty buff paint that had been daubed on over the prize touring car's original colour was still wet to the touch, as I recalled.

Out at the airfield fourteen months later, White-head placed me without difficulty.

"Right over there, detective, with the hole you put in the fender. Quite a feat of marksmanship that! We keep her here now to drive when we hop down to Toronto. Come have a look."

Lucy and I followed to the far side of one of the hangars where a lean-to garage sheltered a lovingly restored pale blue phaeton, parked nose in. There, sure enough, in the right rear fender was the perforation my bullet had made on its way to puncture the tire.

"Thought you'd have fixed it by now," I said.

"Nooo — spoil a good story. Just a touch of paint to keep the rust out and a change of tire. Scars honourably won are nothing to be ashamed of."

"Maisie, meet Wing Commander Christopher Whitehead." I'd warned Lucy we should use one more alias for her until we convinced Whitehead of the need for secrecy.

"First names all round, detective. Call me Kip, Maisie."

"Paul, then." I saw Bea was still chatting gaily and enjoying a donated smoke. "Listen, Kip. We have something important and hush-hush we have to talk to you about before you fly back to Ottawa tonight."

"What the — oh, hello, Clara."

A husky woman in a tweed jacket and jodhpurs had found Kip and wanted to ask him about the tricky business of piloting a plane with a rotary engine. Yes, it was heavy on the controls, but she could handle that. I listened impatiently to her discussing the relationship between temperature and the setting of the air lever at start-up. Kip set her straight on that and went on to warn her of the risk of an over-rich fuel mixture as the r.p.m. increased, this owing to the feeding of the mixture by centrifugal force; he promised to speak to her later. Clara tried to continue the conversation. He then introduced her to "Maisie" and excused himself by saying that after his three-and-a-half-hour flight there were matters he had to attend to without delay. I accompanied him to the latrine.

I told him baldly that the woman he had just met had top secret documents proving that the Germans were building an air force and preparing war against Poland. I added that, although I didn't see how the process could be stopped, it would be a farce to admit Germany to the League of Nations tomorrow.

"Whoa, Paul," Whitehead cut in. He had a basin full of water which he was splashing over his face, his neck, and the grey linoleum floor of the men's washroom. "This sounds nutty as a fruitcake, and I know you're no nut, so we're going to have to take some time to get the story straight."

"We could fill you in while you're eating."

"Bea and I are eating with —"

"There've already been two attempts on her life in Toronto," I said, handing him the damp communal towel. "And one last week in New York. We know another attack is intended. Let Mrs. Whitehead keep the appointment and make your excuses for you. She can say it's air force business, which is no lie."

"I'll tell Clara and Dick myself. Then you two have supper with Bea and me — I tell her everything anyway. If what you say stands up, I'll pursue the thing in Ottawa. And London for that matter. Fair enough?"

The wing commander had made up his mind and took my assent for granted. On the way back to pick up the women, he insisted on talking about how fast Bea had learned to fly since coming to Canada — and not just to fly, but to pilot just about every kind of aircraft ever invented. Her fearlessness in the air amazed him, although she'd been intrepid since he'd first known her as a teenager in Italy. Had I noticed her nose? Not especially, I said — though in truth there *was* something that didn't show in the newspaper photos — a lump, a scar. The signs of an injury imperfectly healed, reminders of adversity survived, made her face less girlish. I could guess what was coming next.

"Mussolini's blackshirt militia broke it," said Kip. "They were going at her father with clubs, three of them, and she jumped in to save him. Hopeless, of course. But what spunk that girl has! It's a mystery to me where she gets it."

Plainly if we wanted Kip, it was the couple or nothing.

The flying club ran a cafeteria, with Irish stew its dish of the day; Kip reserved a meeting room where we could eat in privacy. The walls were painted wartime grey, their only decoration a framed photo of the King and Queen Mary. Two windows faced the airfield, where the last light was draining from the day.

The four of us grouped ourselves around one end of an ink-stained table.

"So, Maisie," said Bea as we settled in, "sounds to me like you're a fellow European. Where are you from?"

"Finland," said Lucy, gamely inventive.

"Gee, that's great. Don't think I've ever met a Finn named Maisie."

"Show Kip the translations," I said.

Kip took from Lucy three pages covered with Ned's schoolboyish handwriting and unfolded them beside his plate.

"These —" He tapped them with his finger. "— are why we changed our supper plans, Bea. Paul says they're evidence that Germany is putting together an illegal air force."

Bea put down her fork, its load of stew untasted. "That would be awful," she said.

Kip didn't answer. He was reading while he ate.

"God," said Bea, "this means war again, doesn't it? With Kip going back to shoot down flyers in Europe and all kinds of people getting killed. Are you sure, Paul, *really* sure it's on the level? How did you folks get this stuff?"

"It's from a Soviet air force officer's briefcase," I said, more to Kip than in answer to Bea's question. "Russia is where Germany is doing its pilot training and test flying, and some of its aircraft manufacture too. They're getting planes from Fokker in Holland as well."

"And I'm betting you're the one that opened that briefcase, Maisie," said Kip, looking up. "Do you have the original documents? With you?"

"Photographs of them."

We had agreed Lucy would wear the bulletproof vest and carry the prints inside it.

"Believe me, Kip," she went on, "they are authentic."

"And did you see this outlaw air force? With your own eyes?"

"I saw the machines. I met the student pilots."

"Then you have to come back to Ottawa with me tonight."

"I could take her in the Bristol," Bea offered. "I'm just ferrying a machine; Kip wants to practise solo night flying." She looked at her husband.

"This takes precedence," he said. "Maisie, have you flown before?"

"In a Junkers Ju-21."

"Crikey!" said Kip. "You're dynamite, my girl. You're coming with me."

"And you with me, Paul?" Bea suggested.

"Heck, no. I'm a Toronto cop. I have to be at my desk bright and early tomorrow morning."

"Then you can have Maisie's luggage sent on to Ottawa for her!" Kip exclaimed.

I liked the way he was throwing himself into the business. After stew and pie had been eaten, and coffee drunk, the wing commander went to make the necessary mechanical adjustments to his Curtiss Canuck. I was bound and determined to see Lucy safely off, but thought in the meantime I might just check back with HQ to see what Linacre had to say about Ewart's gun.

Bea showed me a phone where I could call downtown, then said she'd help Maisie find a flying suit and helmet: was Maisie more Clara's size or Joan's? Joan's suit might be narrow in the shoulders.... The office screen door banged behind the two women and Bea's voice faded into the night.

Although it was after 8:30, Sanderson was still at his desk.

"Reporting from the field?" he said. "I can't see out this courtyard window, Paul, but there must be a blue moon in the sky."

He'd collected three messages to pass on to me. First, Linacre's ballistic tests had shown that the Smith and Wesson Ewart had shot at Lucy was the same gun that had killed Stinson's missus and her boyfriend. I inferred that this revolver was the "material help" Stinson had given Ewart. Curious as I'd been, it was an anticlimax; Stinson couldn't be tried again for the murders he'd committed four years ago.

Then Sanderson surprised me. He'd phoned Lachapelle to see if he could weasel the information I wanted out of the Security Service. Somehow the chemistry between the two inspectors had dissolved a few layers of gluey protocol, and into our lap had fallen this morsel: late last week an RCMP informant had drawn the force's attention to a garage at 468 Manor Road East. On Saturday, a clandestine search had turned up a small supply of explosives, including half a dozen Mills bombs of the type that had gone off in the Beaconsfield Hotel the day before. Everything had been left in place and the premises put under surveillance in the hopes of nabbing anyone visiting the garage to possess himself of the prohibited material.

"Has anyone come?" I asked, wondering about a grenade attack at the airfield.

"Not so far."

"I'd better go, Inspector. I'm at Leaside seeing Lucja Grudzinska off to Ottawa on a plane with Kip Whitehead."

"The fighter ace? Thirty-three kills?"

"That's the one. He believes Lucy's on to something, and he's going to make sure she's heard."

"Glad to hear you'll soon be back to full-time police work. One more thing, Paul: your Detective Mullaney phoned from New York City."

"Important?"

"*I* wouldn't call long distance unless it was, and probably not even then — but maybe his department has a fatter budget. He was replying to the telegram about the Beaconsfield John Doe. Mullaney says they used our information to break open Manfred Krasny, the man from Woolworth's roof. John Doe appears to be his son, real name Victor Krasny. The father was grief-stricken. He said Victor should never have followed your Polish lady north, because whether she used her ticket to Toronto or her ticket to Montreal, agent H. would deal with her."

"Did he say anything more about agent H?"

"Only that, according to Manfred, the Krasnys were bumblers when it came to assassination. But where H. comes from political killings happen all the time."

"Where? Russia?"

"Didn't say."

I rang off then, suddenly needing to clap eyes on Lucy.

I looked first at the hangars. Kip was still at work on the engine of his plane and hadn't seen her, or Bea. Even if he'd glanced out at the airfield, his eyes — accustomed to his array of electric lights — wouldn't have noticed anyone passing. The bonfires, which were to serve as runway lights for the two night take-offs, had not yet been lit; the starlit field was empty. Empty also was the shed where the Hispano-Suiza had been parked. I was pretty worked up now. I ran back to the office and the cafeteria, looking for anyone that might have seen either of the two women. The tall, slim girl named Joan told me she'd heard Bea suggest they drive somewhere to pick up smokes. Lucy had said she'd like a cigarette more than almost anything.

I asked Joan if she had a car I could borrow.

"A Ford pickup. C'mon, I'll drive you."

"Can you drive fast?" A dumb question to ask a flyer, I'll admit.

"You bet! And I know where the store is." Joan's red bob swung from side to side as she raced for the open cockpit of her flivver, parked facing town at the side of McCrae Drive.

I moved to crank the engine for her, but she had an electric starter. I barely made it into the passenger seat before we were off in a cloud of dust from Leaside's unpaved roads. Raising her voice above the engine, Joan asked a lot of questions I didn't answer. She was Bea's friend, after all. I kept saying this all was a police matter and I hoped to be able to tell her more later.

She seemed not altogether sorry that the day's thrills hadn't ended with the day's flying. Still wearing her grease-stained khaki coverall and working the pedals with her flying boots, she swung the throttle lever on the right of the steering column all the way down and left it there. Tools and lumber rattled in the back of the truck whenever we hit a pothole. Speed was for Joan its own justification, I concluded. Telling her I feared a life was in danger wouldn't have got us moving any faster.

We must have driven more than a mile — all the way to Yonge Street. At Joan's suggestion we stopped at both Hooper's Drugs and Knapp's Service Station; no one had seen either of the women we described. The other shops on Yonge between Davisville and Belsize were closed.

"There's nowhere else to buy cigs." Joan turned her long, freckled face my way when we were back in the truck. "What now, copper?"

"Any idea where Manor Road East would be?"

"Sure, a block north of here."

"Number 468," I said.

"That'd be more than halfway back to the airfield."

I nodded. Nothing but swear words were running through my head. Mostly I was cursing myself for letting Lucy out of my sight. The hardest thing for me in the infantry had been living with mistakes that exposed men to unnecessary danger. With a woman, it was worse. No — with *Lucy*, it was worse, far worse. Even though Joan couldn't know all I was thinking, my grimness infected her. She drove without speaking, the drive for her no longer a lark.

Manor Road was paved, so no balloon of dust announced our approach. I had Joan stop three numbers short of 468 and told her to wait in the pickup. It looked as if for once the pavers had got ahead of the builders, for in this block there were still a few vacant lots and houses under construction. Opposite the CPC property stood one of the latter, a half-completed brick shell, with a carpenter's van parked nose in on what would one day be the front lawn. It was from the back of this truck, I reckoned, that the RCMP Security Service would be keeping an eye on things.

The free-standing plank garage of 468 had been built back from the house at the end of a private drive. The house was new and followed a pattern builders were using all over town: full-width front veranda five steps up from yard level; brick first storey; door to one side of the front wall — the right side in this case — and a living room window to the other; roof sloping towards the street with a second-storey dormer for the master bedroom. All the windows were dark with the curtains drawn. There was no car parked in the drive or in front.

If there were people in the house, I could detect no sign. I stole up to the front door and found it locked. The side door too. Time to talk to the Mounties. Crossing the street, I circled the carpenter's van and tapped on the windshield with my badge. No one answered and the doors had been fitted with locks, so I tapped louder, then started banging on the plywood side panels. An out of sorts young man in workman's overalls lowered the driver's side window and pointed a revolver in my face.

"Hands in the air," he hissed. "Drop that."

"Look at it," I said.

"I'm a police officer, and I said — oh, you too. Look, I'm doing a job here for the country. I don't need municipal cops butting in."

Once we'd traded names, I informed RCMP Corporal Shuttleworth that he owed my visit to Inspector Lachapelle. That made me acceptable — up to a point.

"Anyone enter that house in the past hour?" I asked.

"Two women arrived in a luxury car," said the corporal. "The shorter one was dressed like an aviatrix."

"Two women alone? No one else?" I had thought possibly Lucy, with Bea or without, had been abducted by Harbinger and brought here.

"As I said."

Then one of the women had brought the other, and I'd gone too far with Lucy to suspect her of playing a double game.

"Both leave with the car?"

"Come to think of it, only the shorter one."

"How long ago?"

"Not long. It's not my job to watch the house. I just watch the garage, and neither woman went near it. Now if you're finished ..."

"Do you have a two-way radio in your truck?"

"I don't use it. Everyone sounds like he has a mouthful of grass." Shuttleworth did an unnecessary imitation. "I figured if I was going to have to string up an antenna anyway I might as well run a telephone wire up one of the poles. So that's what I did."

"Fine. Phone Leaside airfield and tell them to stop Beatrice Whitehead from flying tonight."

"But —"

"Use all the authority of our two police forces. The woman's a Soviet agent."

"I'd have to ask my —"

"Get officers over there. Then call an ambulance to 468 Manor Road East. I'm breaking into that house, and when you're done phoning I'd appreciate your help."

I wasn't planning on going in quietly, so I hammered the knocker and leaned on the doorbell in case someone inside could save me the mess of breaking glass. It seemed not.

The window in the door was too high up, so I stepped across the veranda to the living room window. My foot was up to kick it in when the front door opened a crack. I plucked my service revolver from its shoulder holster.

"Police! Come out slowly, hands up."

"Paul?" Two syllables, Lucy's voice.

I thanked our stars: she was alive. "Yeah, it's me."

"Ah can't come out." Lucy's voice, but slurred.

"Are you alone?"

"Yes, ah — ah —"

"Hold on."

Stowing my gun, I pushed open the door and found her swaying on her pins. It was too dark to see much, but by the street lamp opposite the front door I could make out that her head and face were bloody. When I'd carried her to a chesterfield in the living room, I turned on an end-table lamp and caught my breath. Blood was coming from at least two blunt-instrument injuries — some from a split in her forehead at the hairline, a lot from a blow across the mouth. Her lips were cracked open; teeth were missing or hanging from bleeding gums. The dental plate was gone. Blood spotted her girdle; her outer garments and the bulletproof vest had been stripped away. Blood was soon spotting the sofa cushions as well. Lucy's head moved woozily from side to side. Her skin was clammy.

"Deep breaths," I said, modelling them. "Keep awake."

"Je-sus!" A woman's voice behind me. "Who did this?"

I looked around and saw my driver hadn't stayed where I'd told her to. Joan had a hand clapped over her mouth; her eyes were wide and brimming. In a flash I believed in her horror and sympathy. Once suckered, you think you'll never trust anyone again, but you do, and already I was doing it.

"Come here, Joan. Keep her conscious. Find out if she has other injuries — besides the ones to her face and head."

"No injury," said Lucy. "But, Paul, the photos — gone!"

Joan knelt by the sofa and took her hand.

"Bea," Lucy stammered, "she has them."

"I got it," I told her. "Hang on. An ambulance is on the way."

I went to look for a dressing for Lucy's forehead and a couple of blankets. I found them all right. I didn't see a phone anywhere, though. Leaving Lucy with Joan, I ran back to Shuttleworth's van. Through his backdoor peephole, he saw me coming. He met me at the cabin door.

"Did you make those calls?" I asked.

"For the ambulance. The rest I'll have to clear with my sergeant. I've left a message for him."

"Hooey."

I'd no time to say more. Plainly, I couldn't expect members of the national police to hop to my orders.

Back in the front room of 468, I told Joan I had to get to Leaside field before the Whiteheads flew out. She said I could have her truck; she'd wait with Lucy for the ambulance.

"Ask them to take her to the Toronto Western." I smoothed Lucy's hair. "See you there, sweetheart. Soon."

"But not before —" She was struggling to remain conscious. Not before I got back her photos: I understood.

At full throttle, the truck felt slower from the driver's seat than from the passenger's side. Add to that the fact that I wasn't as familiar with the maze of Leaside roads as Joan, in consequence missing all the shortcuts to McCrae Drive. When I at last pulled up at the west end of the runway, the bonfires defining its northern and southern edges were lit. I could make out a plane starting to taxi away from me down towards the far eastern end. The engine had a deeper, more powerful voice than the insect hum of the Canuck.

At my end of the runway, not ten yards distant, two men stood smoking pipes and watching the receding plane. I recognized the one in the flat cap as Gus. The tall, blond one was Kip.

"Is that Bea?" I shouted.

Whitehead turned in surprise. "Paul! I wondered where you'd got to."

"Bea?" I asked again, gesturing.

"I wanted her to wait, but they've had the Bristol ready since this afternoon, and she was anxious to get off. Says she'll meet me when we refuel at Kingston."

"Any way to stop her?"

"Stop her?"

"Police business, Kip. Maisie's been attacked."

"Good Lord! Is she all right?"

"I need to keep Bea here."

It was the devil not being able to get the whole nightmare into the doting husband's head in one thrust. When he spoke, it was as an officer, cool in a crisis.

"Bea didn't say anything about an attack. Did you think she might be a witness, Paul? I very much doubt it, but why don't I have her call you from Kingston?"

I grabbed Whitehead's arm. "Is there a radio receiver in the plane?" I asked.

"No." Kip shook his head; his voice got louder. "Paul, what's going on?"

"I have to arrest her," I said.

Gus, who'd been relighting his brier, pricked up his ears.

"Not Bea!" he exclaimed. "Arrest?"

Kip Whitehead was struck dumb. I didn't see the look on his face because I was straining to see Bea's plane by the light of the bonfires. It looked as if it had reached the far end of the runway and was turning around. Suddenly the searchlights at the eastern end of the field went on to illuminate the runway, and I shielded my eyes.

"If we cut power to those lights...?" I said, squeezing Kip's arm again.

"That would put her in danger," Gus volunteered.

"No, no," said Kip. "She won't take off without the lights: I've gone over that with her." He spoke as if in a daze, then pulled himself together. "All right, Gus, do it, but fast."

Gus disappeared into the office block.

"Is there a rifle about?" I asked.

Kip wheeled to face me. "No one is shooting at my wife."

"For the plane, not the pilot," I said. "Kip, listen. If it were just the assault, we could have the police meet her in Kingston. But Bea has the documents — prints and negatives."

He opened his mouth as if to protest, but instead ran off straight down the runway. I followed full tilt into the blinding searchlights. And then the lights went off. I could see nothing, but was hoping to hear the purr of the Bristol engine stop.

It didn't. It stayed constant. Bea must be weighing the odds of taking off safely with only the boundary lights for guidance. I wanted her to stop and think a good long time. But it took her only a moment. The engine noise was coming closer and getting more gas to feed it. Now that my eyes were adjusting, I could make out the Bristol rolling this way as it passed through the light of each of the bonfires in turn. Ahead of me, Kip was still running towards it. Would Bea see him and be able to keep from driving her plane straight into him? I drew my gun.

Kip was waving his arms, but still she came. I veered right and stopped. It was a tricky shot at a moving target, made harder by my heavy breathing, but I had to try. I aimed my service revolver at the nearest tire of the oncoming plane and fired, aiming and firing at the growing target until the cylinder was empty. Despite Kip's kind words about my marksmanship, stopping his Hispano-Suiza had been a piece of cake to this.

I lowered my revolver, fearing to see either the Bristol rising unscathed over my head and away or Kip being mowed down by his wife's propeller. Instead, the plane was turning, spinning around its flat tire. I thought it might tilt it over onto the tip of its right wing, but that didn't happen, perhaps because the engine had by now been cut. I didn't know if Bea had a pistol aboard. I reloaded mine quickly and kept it in my hand.

As soon as the Bristol came to rest, Kip leaped up on the wing. I heard him murmur something to Bea, then take her arm. She slumped forward.

"My God, she's dead." Kip lifted Bea's face between his two hands. "Not a scratch on her, and she's dead. It's not possible."

Chapter 15

EVERYONE REMAINING AT THE airfield had been drawn by the sound of gunfire to Bea's plane. Gus jumped up on the wing and helped Kip lift the pilot out. They laid her on the grass. Kip tried to blow air into her lungs while Gus took Bea's wrist to look for a pulse. I put my revolver back in its holster.

"She's gone, Kip," Gus said at last. His hair tufted up when he pulled off his flat tweed cap.

Kip kept going with the artificial respiration until Gus gently said his name once more. Then he stopped. His back straightened, but he remained on his knees looking down at his love a long moment. Everyone was as still as in a picture — the dead woman stretched on the grass, above her the kneeling figure in the tan flying suit, and the men and women standing around him. The only movement was the flickering play of light from the runway fires.

Then Kip passed his hand over his face and looked around.

"We'll put her in the meeting room." His voice sounded strained but decisive. A number of the bystanders moved to follow him into the office block, but he waved them back. "Could some of you fellows help Moe douse the boundary lights? I won't be flying out tonight."

Clara was carrying an electric torch. I asked if I could borrow it.

"What for?" I couldn't see her expression because she was shining the light in my eyes, but she didn't sound friendly. I showed her my badge.

"Look," I said, "I'm sorry about Bea."

"Funny, isn't it? She's dead, and you were shooting at her — and now you're sorry."

"I didn't kill her, Clara. Ask Kip. We had to stop her."

"With bullets! Why?"

"It's a police matter. I need to have a look inside the cockpit of that machine. Be a peach now and lend me your light."

Clara stood her ground. "This is Leaside, not Toronto. We have our own policeman."

"Call him then; get him over here."

"Nuts to that." She dropped the light from my face and stood with crossed arms in front of Bea's plane.

I tried to rub some of the tightness from my shoulders. I was almost despairing of seeing those air force documents again, but I had to know what had happened to them. I cast about for another way.

Men were using buckets of water and sand to put out the bonfires. A tanker truck drove up and down the runway supplying additional water as required. Asking around, I found that Moe was the guy that had spun the propeller to help Bea start the Bristol. I got him to stop what he was doing and tell me if he'd noticed her carrying an envelope when she climbed into the cockpit.

"Big, brown envelope?" Moe leaned on his shovel and wiped sweat from his forehead with the sleeve of his work shirt. "She had one when we walked to the plane, but she dropped it in one of the bonfires."

"Which one?" I tried to whip some urgency into my voice, though I knew the race was run.

"The Bristol was there." Moe pointed to the nearest hangar. "And we were coming from Kip's hangar. So it must have been —"

I'd followed his reasoning and was already on my way with Moe at my heels. The fire was still burning. By its light I could see the charred corner of an envelope just like the one that had travelled to the airfield inside Lucy's bulletproof vest. While we worked with shovel and sand to get the flames out, Moe delivered his eulogy on Bea.

"She was a great gal, never more than a minute away from smiling. I asked if she was burning love letters. Cheeky of me, 'cause I knew she'd never cheat on Kip. But she played along like a sport. 'Absotively!' she said. 'Top secret romance.'"

I eventually got a lamp from Moe and went through the embers. I found a little crumb of what looked like celluloid film. I could have asked Dalton Linacre to take a look, but there was no hope of reconstructing the negatives. The prof had enough work of the kind that can change the outcome of a trial. Confirming my despair would have been a waste of his time. When Clara tired of standing guard on the Bristol, I had a thorough look through it — and the Hispano-Suiza too for good measure. I found no further trace of the documents Lucy had risked so much for.

A light was still burning in the office. The pale, paunchy man I'd heard called Dick was on the desk phone. Rather than flying gear, he wore a short-sleeved white shirt open at the neck, dark flannels, and a pencil behind the ear. I took him for the airport manager. He was explaining that Daddy had been kept late, but would read the next chapter of *Doctor Dolittle* as soon as he got home. When he hung up, I asked him if Bea had made any calls just before getting in her plane. He looked up at me from his swivel chair. He said she had, quite a short one. I asked what she'd said. Word had got around that I was a cop. Dick answered without making difficulties.

"She said, 'I found your pearls.'"

"What else?" I asked. "Try to give the whole of her side of the conversation, just as you heard it."

Dick dropped his head and pinched the bridge of his nose. "As near as I can recall, she said, 'Iris, it's me.' She didn't say her name, just, 'It's me.' Then, 'I found your pearls.... You can stop looking for them; they're perfectly safe.... I'll tell you the whole story when I'm back in Ottawa.' There might have been a *goodbye* or a *cheerio* at the end. Otherwise, that's it."

"What number did she call?"

Dick had no idea. Bea had dialed it herself.

"'Stop looking,'" I said. "You're sure you heard those words?"

"One hundred per cent, detective. I could hear her quite clearly. She didn't ask me to leave the office or try to keep her voice down or anything. Everything open and above board, just the way it always was with Bea. That's why it's so hard for any of us to make sense of what went on tonight. Even if you're not authorized to explain it now, will it all be coming out in the papers at least?"

I told Dick I couldn't promise him that and asked to use the phone. The Toronto Western Hospital would tell me no more than that a patient named Lucy Clarkson had been seen by an emergency room doctor and admitted. I got nothing about her condition. The call made me desperate to get downtown.

But I had to finish up here first.

I asked Dick if he had any way of making a cup of tea before I tackled Kip. He was sorry, no. No refrigerator either, although there was a carton of O'Keefe's ginger ale in a back corner under a table covered with maps. I took a couple of warm pint bottles with me.

Gus was standing guard at the closed door of the meeting room. "He wants to be alone with her," he said.

I told him I was sorry. He didn't block my way.

The room was dark. I closed the door behind me. By the light of the night sky out the windows I saw Bea laid out on the ink-stained table where we'd eaten supper. Beside her lay a wrench, which I assumed had been in the pocket of her flying suit.

Kip followed my eyes. "It has blood on it," he said numbly. "Whose, Paul?"

While in his heart he must have known, he seemed to need the answer to come from outside.

"Maisie's," I said. "Her real name is Lucy."

"Is she dead?"

"She's in the hospital. I don't know how badly she's hurt."

"Why did Bea do it?"

I told him. I don't think he took much of it in. He sat staring like a victim of combat shock. When I'd finished, he spoke in the same monotone as before.

"She poisoned herself. I smelled the cyanide on her breath."

I let that lie.

He noticed my silence and pulled himself together enough to look at me. "Good shooting, Paul. You couldn't have known this would be the result."

Gallantry even in grief — that was the quality of the man. Having seen Dan Ewart's death, however, I couldn't hear Kip's reassurance with a totally clear conscience. Knowing as I now did that the negatives had never been in Bea's plane, I wished we'd let her go.

"You must be exhausted," I said. "Why don't you get some rest?"

It sounded as fatuous to me as it must have to Kip. On second thought, I don't think he even heard me.

"She had too much fun to have been a Marxist," he protested. There was a catch in his voice now. He was fighting his way past the shock, opening himself up to sharper hurt. "Marxists are dead against enjoying anything that everybody can't have." He paused to scrape together his thoughts. "No lobster for anyone till there's enough to go round. Am I right?"

I said I didn't know.

"Well, Bea was no snob, but boy did she know how to live the good life! She loved jewellery, cocktails, perfume, high-heeled shoes...." Kip lost himself a moment in remembering Bea's many pleasures. "From what I've seen," he pushed on, "political women are humourless scolds. Bea wasn't like that."

"No," I said. "I know she wasn't."

"And she wasn't suicidal."

"Not in the normal run of things. But this was different."

"How?" Kip leaned forward in his chair and spread his arms above the figure dimly outlined on the table. *"How* can you make sense of this?"

The skinned-alive agony in his voice drove it home that nothing I could say would meet his need for answers. Not tonight — possibly not ever. Still, he was practically begging me.

I put it out that Bolshevik Russia believed — like any nation — that it needed every kind of support, the secret agent no less than the open propagandist. The OGPU was, for all intents and purposes, a military unit with its own duties and discipline. Part of that discipline was telling no tales.

"But look, Paul, Russia's a dictatorship. Bea hated dictators. Look at the trouble she got into with Mussolini."

"From what I hear, Mussolini's none too gentle with Communists. Heck, Kip, you know the layout better than I do."

"She never told me."

"Would you have married her if she had?"

"She let me think she was fighting for freedom, for free speech." Again his voice was wobbling. "You were out there tonight, Paul. You think she would have run me down?"

"Not on purpose. She was counting on getting airborne before you got too close."

"But is it possible she never loved me?"

I hoped Kip was talking to himself. I barely knew the woman.

"What's your opinion?" Kip persisted.

"Really, I —"

"An outside view."

"Does love have to be all or nothing? If — in three years of marriage — you never suspected otherwise, I say she loved you. At the same time, her loyalties were split. I imagine leaving you the way she did took every ounce of discipline she possessed."

I wasn't making excuses for Bea. She'd belonged to a gang that had tried to kill Lucy in order to conceal plans for aggressive war. Maybe at one time back in Italy the young Bea had been as romantic and idealistic as Lucy in Russia. Bea, however, had clung unswervingly to her faith even when it betrayed its internationalist promise, even when it required her to break heads. And Bea had against our best efforts won the day. I had reason enough to hate her — but no heart for trying to make the man whose ring I saw shining in the starlight on her dead finger hate her too.

Kip seemed to be staring at the ring as well. For a long time, neither of us spoke. Then I used the edge of the table to pry open the ginger ale bottles and passed him one. He took a gulp.

"You taste the sugar more when they're not chilled."

The commonplaceness of Kip's remark encouraged me to ask a loose-end tying question. "What did she tell you when she came back to the airfield without Lucy?"

"Lucy? Oh, Bea said she'd dropped her at a car stop on Yonge Street. She said Maisie had got nervous about flying and decided to go up to Ottawa on the train tomorrow."

Kip gave me back the translations. I asked if he reckoned they'd be of any use on their own, but he said he couldn't think about that now. He told me to go see how Lucy was. It sounded like good advice. I had just one more unpleasant thing to say first.

"There'll have to be an autopsy done, Kip. I'll have Bea picked up. Meanwhile, why don't you let the guys sit with you?"

I handed my untasted ginger ale to Gus on the way out. In the open cockpit of the Ford pickup, the night air whistling past my ears, I felt a kind of freedom — freedom to think of nothing but Lucy. I ran red lights. I couldn't have driven more impatiently if I'd had better news to tell. I just wanted to see her.

It was after ten by the time I parked outside the Western. They told me Lucy had been transferred to the women's ward on the second floor. Jane Sparrow intercepted me in the doorway, her square jaw set. In hushed tones she conveyed the unsurprising information that visiting hours had ended long ago. Could an exception not be made for Lucy Clarkson's nearest and dearest? One already had, Nurse Sparrow informed me. For Lucy's sister Joan, who was keeping quiet vigil at the bedside. I asked to speak to Joan, who was sent out to me in the second-floor hall.

The skin under Joan's eyes was dark. She attempted a greeting, which got smothered by a yawn. She sank onto the other end of the slat-back wooden bench on which I was perched.

"Thanks for waiting," I said.

"Come off it! I couldn't go without my truck."

"How is she?"

"They say the second concussion in less than a week carries a risk of complications. What's that mean? Posing as her sister, I couldn't very well ask."

"She had a door fall on her last Friday," I said. "Her life's not in danger, is it?"

"Not critical danger, they tell me, or they wouldn't leave her here in the ward. They're letting her sleep now, and her pulse is ticking over sweetly." Joan leaned forward, her elbows on her knees, and dropped her voice to a whisper. "You think Bea meant to kill her?"

"I doubt it. Look, you've already been more than swell, but I have to ask you for one more favour: don't spill anything you've seen or heard tonight to the newshounds. Forget the address you drove me to. Let the police tell the story; you don't know all the angles."

"No guff I don't!" The young pilot slid closer down the bench; she kept her voice low but insistent. "I've shared flying tips and ice cream cones with Bea Whitehead, a toothbrush too from time to time. I just can't believe the things I've been hearing about her tonight."

"You're not alone."

"Well, flatfoot, now is the later when you were going to tell me more. Fill me in and I'll know just what not to tell the reporters."

"Bare bones then. Your 'sister' Lucy had something Bea wanted."

"Photos, the way I heard it."

"Okay, photos. Bea brought her to Manor Road to take them from her. Once she had them, leaving Lucy dead would have caused Bea problems. She'd been seen leaving the airfield with Lucy."

"Wasn't she afraid Lucy would tell the cops?"

"Lucy's an illegal alien; as the wife of an ace pilot, Bea's practically royalty. Lucy alive with a concussion might have been dealt with once Bea was back in Ottawa and had had time to prepare Kip."

I was levelling with Joan. In my head, I played over the line I thought Bea might have taken —

That Maisie or whatever she calls herself is bats. Her chatter about all those secret airplanes fooled me at first, but didn't add up when I thought it over. Then a bump on the head must have knocked a few more of her screws loose. She hadn't a mark on her when I left her at the car stop, but I guess she walked into traffic and got run into. Now of all things the poor duck imagines I biffed her.

The delivery would have been fast and frank-sounding with a roll of the eyes, a shrug of the shoulders, a toss of the blond head in all the right places to put the words over. It seemed to me Bea might have brazened it out.

"So letting Lucy live had nothing to do with qualms of conscience," said Joan.

"Maybe secondarily." I suspected Bea's conscience would have told her to stomp on any qualms that didn't serve the cause.

"Those photos must be doozies. Was Lucy using them for blackmail?"

I couldn't let the imputation stand. "Not at all."

"Photos she knew Bea wouldn't want Kip to see?" Joan persisted. "Affairs of the heart."

"Kip saw them."

"Affairs of the heart — or of the bedroom?"

"Affairs of state," I said. "Politics." In the past five days politics had grown in my understanding from a marginal pastime and a topic banned from dinner conversation into what people meant by justice and what they felt for home. "Of the heart, maybe, too," I added. "The political heart."

A nurse carrying a tray of medicines came padding up the grand staircase on crepe-soled shoes and disappeared into the ward — intending, no doubt, to wake patients up so they could take their sleeping draughts. I wondered if Lucy needed morphine, thought she'd prefer vodka.

"Guess I never really knew Bea," Joan said. "I thought I did, but when you come down to it, we never talked about what we believed — except what we thought the weather would be doing by the time we wanted to take off. When she was in town, we were just flygirls together. Did you arrest her?"

"She's dead, Joan."

"Holy cow! You might have said so sooner."

I didn't argue with that.

"What did she die of?" Joan studied my face.

I met her eyes, trying to make up with a direct look for an evasive answer. "There'll be an autopsy."

"Come on," she said through clenched teeth. "How did it happen?"

I told her what everyone at the airfield had seen, without mentioning the word suicide. Privately, I speculated that when Bea was stopped on the runway the brazen-it-out strategy had looked a lot more dubious. Maybe she panicked. Maybe she was following secret agent protocol: never let them take you alive. Or perhaps she just couldn't bear to face the man that had given her his name, his country, and his love.

"Bea Whitehead dead." Joan took a deep breath. "A more seasoned pilot might have been fast enough on the rudder to keep the plane straight."

"And headed straight for Kip," I said. "Either she meant to spare him or it was a good thing for him he hadn't taught her everything he knew. Now you scamper on home before you're too bushed to drive."

"Did you get the photos back?"

I shook my head and told her she'd find her truck on the far side of Bathurst Street by a fire hydrant. After she'd gone, I stretched out and fell asleep myself on the bench where we'd been sitting — until Jane Sparrow came and threw me out.

It was tough leaving without so much as a glimpse of Lucy. At the same time, I trusted Nurse Sparrow to keep her alive for me, and I still had work at City Hall. Back at my desk, I got the telephone company to tell me what number Bea had dialed from the airfield. It turned out to belong to an apartment-dweller in the Beach neighbourhood, so I had Station Number Eight send a constable to investigate. I wanted whoever had taken Bea's call, whether named Iris or not, held for questioning.

By now the graveyard shift had taken over the office. One detective had his head down on his desk; another looked to be busy over some paper, which turned out to be a crossword puzzle; two more were quietly discussing the Cardinals' chances of winning their first pennant. They sounded well-informed, so I got one of them to tell me the name of the Leaside policeman and where I'd find his phone number. I gave Sandy Bruce a ring to let him know I'd been on his turf and to clear with him the removal of Beatrice Whitehead's body from the airfield. Then I bummed a stick of Wrigley's from the puzzler in the hopes that chewing on it would keep me awake long enough to fill in the form required whenever an officer's firearm is discharged. By the time I'd cleaned my service revolver, I knew I was in no shape to type a full report. It crossed my mind to ask for a bunk in the police lock-up, but just then the constable from Number Eight phoned in to say there was no one home at the

"Iris" apartment. I was ready for a hot shower and my own bed. I told him not to wait and caught the last Queen car westbound.

Chapter 16

UNTYPICALLY, I BOUGHT A *Star* next morning — Wednesday, September 9. I told the newsboy I was supporting the strikers by boycotting the scab edition of the *Examiner*. Something else was at work, though. The *Examiner* wasn't much for international news at the best of times, and I needed to torment myself with the headlines out of Europe:

WORLD-WAR FEUDS DIE AS
GENEVA OPENS DOOR AND BIDS
BERLIN ENTER

Former Foes Extend Hand of Welcome
by Unanimous Vote Today

Germany's Envoys Leave for Geneva
to Sit in League

I'd had more than enough of the gushing Associated Press dispatches by the time my car reached Bathurst Street, so I jumped off and walked up to Dundas. It was nine a.m. when I got there. I was already late for work, but too early for Western Hospital visiting hours — as Daisy Bennett was not shy about informing me.

"Old friends can bend the rules a bit," I suggested.

"Nothing doing." The young nurse glared owlishly at me through the round lenses of her new glasses. "However, the doctor has seen Miss Clarkson this morning and authorized her discharge. If you bring her some clothes while she has her bath, you can not only see the Throttler but take her." Benny struggled with a smile and vanquished it. "Just remind her to settle her hospital bill before leaving, will you? She owes the Western now for two admissions, plus an ambulance."

I guessed Lucy's green dress was too badly ripped to wear. I got her raincoat from my apartment and took her back there. I was gambling that Bea's "stop looking" message had ended the hunt for Lucy. In the light of day, I appreciated Bea's having taken time to make the phone call — though that appreciation wasn't nearly enough to let me forgive her for the brutal job she'd made of Lucy's face.

Her mouth was a heartbreak to look at — misshapen from the lack of teeth and swollen with bruises. She mumbled a droll warning against trying to make her laugh — then gave me a teasing hug and sent me back to work, with a request that I bring home something to drink.

At HQ, I ran into Ned Cruickshank, groggy after his night of following Stinson around. He said Harbinger had never shown up, but while waiting and watching he'd had an idea. We'd been thinking in terms of *he* and *him*. What if Harbinger were a woman? Why yes, I agreed, this very thought had recently crossed my mind. Then I got Ned to phone Snodgrass and ask the prof if he could vouch for the authenticity of the documents we'd had him translate.

The events of the previous evening weren't going to give rise to any criminal charges: Lucy's assailant was beyond the reach of the law. HQ was nonetheless left with the question of what to feed the news organizations. Clara Bain and other members of the Toronto Flying Club had already spoken to reporters from the Toronto dailies, who were now phoning City Hall for corroboration, refutation, background, foreground, and comment. Sanderson felt duty-bound to consult the RCMP Security Service on the management of these inquiries, and the Mounties weren't slow to make their wishes known.

I was commanded to another interview with Inspector Claude Lachapelle early that afternoon. He reminded me that I owed him the tip about the property on Manor Road. I thanked him. He cautioned me that the address must on no account become public knowledge as long as the premises remained under surveillance. Fair enough, I thought. He had other demands, however. He wanted to see or hear nothing in the news about Soviet agents in connection either with Mrs. Whitehead's passing or with Dan Ewart's.

Or, for that matter, with that of the Beaconsfield bomber, now identified as Victor Krasny. The latter two deaths were to be attributed to bungled attempts at armed robbery. Out of consideration for her husband — a hero to many if no more than a stunt flyer to the inspector — Beatrice Whitehead would be reported as having succumbed to a heart attack. Cyanide was not to be mentioned, whatever the autopsy showed. As for the use of firearms, I had shot her plane's tire out merely to prevent what could, given the malfunction of the searchlights, have been an unsafe takeoff.

I replied that it wasn't my job to brief members of the press — and fortunately not, as I'd have no part in spreading these fairy tales. Nor need I, Lachapelle assured me. All that was required was that I not contradict them. My final words to the inspector were that I reserved my right to spread news of the Russo-German arms buildup, cost what it cost me. As long as I spoke of treaty violations in Europe as opposed to crimes in Toronto, Lachapelle expressed himself confident that my efforts would be without either cost or benefit.

I came home to find Lucy had acquired a radio and a new rose-coloured frock with long sleeves, a low waist, and fancy embroidery around the collar. I'd had no idea they sold such things in my neighbourhood. I thought it must have taken a lot of courage for Lucy with her bruised and stitched-up face to approach the sales clerks, but she made light of that: was the war so long ago I'd forgotten what bravery was? She'd also bought me a steak which I fried with onions and masticated shamelessly while she sipped bouillon spiked with rye. After dinner, she took off her frock to show me some new underwear. When I'd said my two words about that, she took off her underwear, and we made love. She warned me not to expect much in the way of kissing or biting, but urged me to go all out — not to treat her as fragile.

"I know you're tough as a rhino," I said, "but if I feel like being tender you'll just have to take it."

We took our time and lay together a long time afterwards. Then we poured ourselves tumblers of whisky and Lucy mumbled out all she could recollect of the sorry story of the previous evening.

She couldn't explain why she hadn't been suspicious of Bea Whitehead. It wasn't just that I'd vouched for Kip and Kip trusted Bea. It wasn't just that Lucy was more used to dealing with duplicitous men than with treacherous women. It wasn't just the carefree, fun-loving personality Bea projected. Nor yet was it the fact that, for all her verve and aviatrix sportiness, Bea appeared soft and unmuscular — no match for Lucy in combat. It was none of these, but some of each plus — what? Mesmerism? No, it wasn't to be explained, but when Bea suggested they drive out for cigarettes in the powder blue phaeton, Lucy went.

She thought it odd that Bea should drive them to a house rather than to a store, but Bea assured her this was a house she often slept in when she was staying over in Toronto — and much closer than the store. Bea had a key. She led the way inside. Lucy might have been wary if Bea had expected her to go first. In the living room, Bea told Lucy to look through the drawers of a writing desk for smokes while Bea checked a cabinet under the bookcase. Lucy bent over the desk, but sensed a quick movement behind her and turned her head just in time to catch the blow from Bea's wrench in the mouth instead of on the cranium. From here on, Lucy's memory was cloudy. She was pretty sure she'd spat out a tooth and felt blood dribble down her chin. She thought she'd landed a few kicks, but Bea had managed to stay on her feet.

The problem was that Bea still had the wrench and could wield it with either hand. Lucy was backed into a corner. She couldn't run. She couldn't reach any object that might serve her as a weapon. Her padded vest, while it absorbed a couple of slashing blows, limited her agility. The last thing she could picture was herself lunging for Bea's right wrist, and the wrench thrown from Bea's right hand to her left. That's when Bea must have got in the crack on the skull she had been aiming for. Lucy went down, and out.

And the photographs? Bea had probably — Lucy and I agreed — learned from Harry North about the two failed searches in London and concluded that Lucy had a way of keeping the film with her, but not in her clothes. Perhaps Bea would have come on her own to the idea of checking for false teeth, but her wits were never tested to that extent. The blow to Lucy's face had broken the dental plate, and part of it had come out of her mouth. The layers of Vulcanite may have become separated. To find film hidden between them as Lucy lay unconscious would have been quick and easy. Bea needed the prints too, but they were large and easily located under Lucy's vest.

Lucy had come to in a silent house, still too queasy to move. But then she heard someone try the door. She didn't know it was me, but surely anyone that was coming to harm her would have a key. When I began pounding on the door, she dragged herself to her feet … and I knew the rest.

Lucy didn't have to ask if I'd recovered the photos. But she wanted to hear what had become of them and of Bea. So I told her all that and the day's news from Geneva as well. Over a couple more drinks, I promised to do what I could with the translations. And suggested Lucy see what sort of stir her news might make in the city's Polish community.

This was something she'd set out to do on her first weekend in Toronto. To find where in Toronto her countrymen had clustered, she'd looked up common Polish names in the city directory: Nowak, Kowalski, Jaworski — as well as their New World respellings with *v* in place of *w*. Calling on one of these had led her to the temptation of easy money and to the rigged card game she'd already mentioned. This time I was able to direct her to St. Stanislaus Church, which was practically on my streetcar ride to work. Lucy spoke to the priest and to two or three of the leading parishioners. Pickings were sparse. Winnipeg, not Toronto, was the largest centre of Polish-Canadian life. She was told that Russo-German hostility to the homeland came as no surprise, but that there were no members of the provincial legislature or of the federal parliament that could be brought to take the threat seriously. And since she had no proof ... A shrug, a sigh — the rest went without saying.

I fared no better with my MP. "A vast ocean separates us from Europe," he quoted our Canadian delegate to the League as saying — and the ocean only seemed to have grown vaster in the eight years since the war. Where was Poland, anyway? Russia was to be feared, certainly, but as a source of socialist ideology rather than of military force. Policing the terms of the Versailles Treaty was a matter the member was content to leave to Whitehall. Even if Great Britain got sucked into another war on the continent, that wouldn't implicate this country, not the way it had in 1914 when we'd been no more than a colony. And since I had no proof ...

Proof wasn't something Snodgrass was able to provide. His specialty was Leo Tolstoy, and he'd been under the impression that the pages Ned and Lucy had brought him had been part of a novel. Needless to say, I didn't quote the good professor when I wrote to our prime minister and to members of the British government. None of these letters was answered.

One letter surprisingly did bring something in return. Nick Mazur — the Polish-American that Lucy had tried to connect with at the Woolworth Building — remembered Mary Kaminska's missed appointment on September 1. He wrote that he'd been curious about what had happened to her, all the more so because of the unusual incident that day of the man on the roof. I'd given Mazur the dirt on the German air force and asked him if he thought the United States government might pick up the ball. On that point, he wrote:

> *As a Pole born and bred, and a proud American today, I wish I had sunnier news for you. My business at* Public Voice *magazine is measuring public opinion. We conduct surveys and often manage to predict the outcome of elections. Sometimes we get things wrong. Still, I'm going to stick my neck out and predict what American public opinion will be the week German and Russian forces invade Poland. The president, whoever he is, whichever party he represents, will declare American neutrality and his resolve to keep the United States out of the fighting. At least four out of five Americans will condemn the aggressors. The* New York Times *will go so far as to suggest that if the English and the French are drawn into the conflict we eventually may be also. But all will agree to delay taking up arms just as long as possible. By then, of course, it will be too late to save Poland.*

It was ten days before Lucy's mouth was healed enough for her to see a dentist about new bridgework.

We wasted more time than I care to remember cursing fate. Generally, though, we ran away from the blues just as hard and as fast as we could. I had a telegram from Hasty MacDermid inviting me out to the fall fair in Streetsville to see his fire extinguisher demonstration. I replied that I looked forward to standing him a drink next time he was back in Toronto, but that I had no desire to see anything in flames, not even as part of a show.

At night Lucy and I were burning up the sheets and drinking a regiment's ration of hard liquor, while during the day I went to City Hall and buried myself in the assignments given me. Inspector Sanderson, at his most priest-like, asked me if I was cohabiting with the Polish woman. I saw in his eyes that he desperately wanted to be lied to. I obliged.

One evening, Dot dropped by the apartment. The radio was playing "No, No, Nanette," as it often did, and I missed the knock on the door. Lucy opened and the two made their own introductions. Lucy smiled and apologized for her busted up mouth. She had a drink in her hand, which she offered to Dot. Dot shook her head; she looked small and nervous and as pale as her white sailor's middy. I was making scrambled eggs for supper, something that didn't need chewing, and it was easy to add a couple more to the bowl. Dot was reluctant, but in the end agreed to eat with us. She latched onto the radio and ran through every station on the dial until she was feeling less shy.

"So are you two lovers?" she blurted out when we were all sitting down.

"Funny," Lucy said with a friendly smile. "I was going to ask you and Paul the same thing."

Dot took some bread. "Don't I wish!"

"Lucy's the one that got hit by the door in the Beaconsfield explosion," I said chattily.

"Gee. That must have terrified the bejesus out of you."

I could see Lucy didn't know the expression. "She says you must have been very scared."

"I would say I was angry. Scared? Not very — maybe more when I was younger."

"How old are you?" said Dot. "If you don't mind my asking."

"I don't mind. I'm twenty-six."

I thought Lucy had to be fibbing. She had impersonated the thirty-six-year-old Edna Salisbury, and I hadn't thought she was many years younger than that. If she were telling the truth, she'd been in prison and had run away from home at sixteen. She had fought through the Russian Revolution in 1917 and the following Civil War before she was twenty. She was as old and as young as the century.

"Twenty-six, eh? I'm twenty-three today, so there's not that much difference between us. See Paul rolling his eyes? He doesn't believe me, but today I brought proof."

Out of her purse, Dot pulled a graduation photo. Four rows of children stood in a schoolyard. Three of the kids sitting in the front row held a sign that read: *Grade VIII Class of 1917*. Standing in the second row, probably because she was shorter than the student behind, was Dot. She showed us her driver's permit for good measure.

"It's true you look younger," said Lucy. "But you still have time to make your dreams come true."

I didn't ponder what she might mean by this. My thoughts were on the Old World where people had to grow up so quickly, and the New World where we didn't have to grow up at all, neither our flappers nor our statesmen.

Friday I got paid. So on Saturday I gave Lucy her first exposure to baseball, at the new Maple Leaf Stadium down by the lake. Getting off the Bathurst car, we saw a well-dressed girl chaining an expensive new bike to a hydro pole. She was using one of those Danziger keyless padlocks my colleague Rudy Crate had shown me; I told her she should buy something more secure.

"That so?" she said. "Well, I can't stop now. It's my brother's first start as pitcher."

Lucy was a good sport about sitting on hard seats in the hot sun. She was bored, though, as anyone is likely to be at their first ball game. So even though some tricky pitching by our friend's brother had kept the score tied, we left to get ourselves a drink at the end of six innings. Strolling back to the car stop with our arms around each other's waists, damned if we didn't spot some scamp in plus fours popping the lock on sis's bike. He paused only half a second when I yelled at him to stop in the name of the law or some fool thing. But that half second cost him. He missed a gap in the traffic on Lakeshore Boulevard, then couldn't get across. By now I was running full tilt. I still shouldn't have caught him: all I can think is that the girl's machine was too small for him and that her under-inflated tires were a drag on his speed. As he stood pumping the pedals for dear life, I leaped at him in a sort of flying tackle and brought him down. It put a good scare into him, but apart from scratches on his cheek and hand and a little paint chipped off the new bike no harm was done. I felt good. I hadn't had enough of this kind of exercise lately.

Of course, then we had to take bike and thief to a police station. Lucy hung around while paperwork was done and was sweet enough not to mention her thirst more than twice. Fanning herself with her programme, she was also the one to suggest that we'd have no trouble finding the bicycle's owner if — that is — she really was the pitcher's sister.

This weekend arrest, I should point out, had nothing to do with busting the gang of bike rustlers. That nab was made thanks to Ned Cruickshank, who took it on himself to stake out the best of the decoys Crate had wangled, and to watch it night and day until it was loaded into a van Ned could take the plate number of. I recommended Cruickshank for promotion. Sanderson said he'd take the matter under advisement.

Ned was also the man that caught up with Iris, in reality a CPC member named Theo de Jong. De Jong claimed he'd been instructed to forward all Iris messages by telegram to an address in London, England. Whether Scotland Yard's Special Branch ever tied that address to Harry North I didn't hear.

I left some time, but not enough, after Bea's death before telegraphing Kip in Ottawa about the German air force. He didn't reply. I tried again a week later with the same result. And then finally, in October, he phoned me long distance at City Hall. He said that without the photos the translations would be unpersuasive and that he, in any case, would for personal reasons have to bow out of the business.

That sounded callous to me. Not callous like Bea swinging her wrench, but complacent as regards the coming conflagration in Europe. On reflection, I thought better of him — as a decent man blinded by love, and now suffering the consequences. Not hard-hearted, rather too tender-hearted to have been properly curious. He'd told me it was a mystery to him where Bea got her spunk. Not every man is made for solving mysteries. I'd already read that he had abandoned the idea of flying to the Arctic and was spending any time he could spare from the RCAF on charitable work for the Anglican church.

At the beginning of December, when the first snowflakes of the winter were falling, I remembered the night clerk, Alex Horvath, and wrote Kip to ask him if he'd like to meet the Hungarian pilot he'd donated his flying gloves to. The fighter ace replied that he'd rather not, that anything associated with his Italian days was painful to him.

By this time, of course, Lucy was long gone.

The day she got her new teeth, we drank bubbly smuggled in from Quebec and danced at the Palais Royale to the music of Harold Rich. Lucy's new mouth was less distinctive than her old: the teeth stretched the lips differently. But kissing and biting no longer posed a problem. Her English was just about perfect by this time, and she'd even taught me to recognize one or two Polish endearments.

Next evening was less of a good time. I knew something was up when I got home — a way of referring to my apartment I was just getting used to — and found Lucy had the radio off. She said we were out of hooch. I didn't buy that, but decided I'd let it lie till after supper. After supper, she sat me up on the bed, with my back against the headboard and snuggled down beside me with my arm around her shoulders, hers around my waist.

"Paul."

"Don't," I said. "I'll do everything necessary for you to stay in the country."

"Those are good words to hear."

"Stay then."

I felt her head shake against my chest. Just under my nose, her wavy hair shook too, releasing a smell not of shampoo but of her. A perfume I hadn't got nearly enough of.

"I don't think I can do without you," I said.

"You can."

"Why even try, Lucy?"

"I care for you too. Believe me, *kochanie*. I arrived in your country alone. You helped me...."

"Look, sister, I believed in what you were trying to do. Spare me your gratitude."

She held me tighter.

"Was sharing a bed just your way of saying thanks?" If I was trying to start a fight — and at that moment I was too unhappy to know what the hell I was doing — it wasn't working.

"No, Paul," she said in a small, soft voice. "I fell for you."

"Like you fell for Harry."

"Harry? Harry was good for a cup of tea, but he felt nothing for me as a woman. Besides, it was weak of him to give me money and let me go. You are different."

"Yeah, ruthless. Ha-ha! If I say you're staying, you're staying."

"You won't say that."

I thought I practically had. I adjusted my right arm so I could stroke her hair. "Why, Lucy?" I murmured.

"I failed —"

"We failed."

"No, Paul, *I* lost the photos. I failed my country again. Maybe I was stupid; maybe one woman could not save Poland. But now I have to go back and share the suffering. You are in my heart, Paul, but so is my country. I have been such a bad Pole, fighting even against my own family, and I feel I only have one more chance to be — not good, but just okay."

I remembered what I'd told Kip about love and divided loyalties.

"Still," I said, "you could stay a little longer. We never had that walk in the park at sunrise. Wait till the leaves turn colour; the red and gold will take your breath away. Heck, wait till spring. We can go skating this winter on Grenadier Pond."

"No, now is a good time. I have just enough money left for my steamer passage. If I wait any longer, I'll have started a job and bought all kinds of clothes and things; I'll have had so many more wonderful times with you, and it will just be harder to leave." Suddenly she lifted her head, and her magnificent grey eyes searched my face. "Will you come with me?"

The fantasy lasted about as long as a soap bubble. I wanted Lucy. But I also wanted to work in my own language in my own country at a job I believed I could do and could even get better at. In Poland, all I could do was fight when the time came, if I wasn't too old. I might not even be able to keep Lucy safe.

"No, Lucy, I can't — and I don't like the idea of your going back into harm's way either." Lucy's impulses had so often worked against her and against what she was trying to do that I wanted her to think this return to Poland over from top to bottom. "Poles emigrate all the time," I reasoned. "Ask anyone you like — it wouldn't be wrong for you to stay with me."

"I've made many mistakes, my love, but this time I'm sure I know the right thing without asking. I have to be in Warsaw when the bombs start to fall."

And she was.

The End

Author's Note

LIKE ALL THE CHARACTERS in this book, Lucy is fictitious. What she says about German rearmament, however, is true. A flying school and test pilot facility were set up in Lipetsk, Russia, to enable Germany to build an illegal air force. Warplanes for Germany were manufactured in a number of countries — including Russia, where there was a Junkers factory. Existence of such facilities was not public knowledge in September 1926 when Germany was admitted to the League of Nations.

And it's surprising how long the secret has lasted. These treaty violations had been written of repeatedly by the time I attended high school in the 1960s, but were still absent from the curriculum. The textbook view then — held by many still — was that the "unwise, unimaginative, and vengeful terms of the Versailles Treaty were largely responsible for the conditions that were to bring about a second world war" (Peart and Schaffter, *The Winds of Change*).

Indeed, the Versailles demands for high reparation payments from Germany did cause bitterness and ill will, but that's only half the story. As regards the re-establishment of the German military, the case of Lipetsk suggests the Allies weren't too exigent in the demands they made at Versailles but rather too lax in seeing that those demands were met. Historian Hew Strachan writes, "Liberalism's comparative failure in the inter-war years was in large part due to its own fundamental decency. It lost the determination to enforce its own standards."

Acknowledgements

I AM GRATEFUL TO a number of people whose brains I have picked to make this work of fiction as authentic as possible. Let me acknowledge here the valuable contributions of Steve Jobbitt, Mary Helen Kaizer, Tom Wood, and Richard Lane. *Fire on the Runway* has also benefited from the literary advice of Lesley Mann and Robert Ward. This novel started down the road to publication with Napoleon & Company, which subsequently merged with Dundurn Publishing. The support of both firms has been invaluable. Special thanks to Sylvia McConnell and Allister Thompson. Finally, love and gratitude to the critical reader with whom I share my life and to whom this novel is dedicated, Carol Jackson.

More by Mel Bradshaw

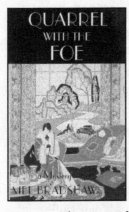

Quarrel With the Foe
A Paul Shenstone Mystery
978-1894917285
$18.95

After surviving the horrors of the Great War, Paul Shenstone works as a police detective in 1920s Toronto, rooting out petty criminals and rum-runners. The unusual murder of a prominent industrialist gives him the biggest case of his career and a not entirely welcome opportunity to make his name on the force. The waters are muddied when the investigation starts uncovering connections between the deceased Digby Watt and soldiers Shenstone knew in Flanders. What will Shenstone's choice be if he has to arrest one of his own comrades? He has promised Watt's attractive and independent daughter that he will bring the perpetrator to justice, but bonds forged in war are not easily broken. In the end, what does justice require, restitution or punishment?

"... vividly written, tightly plotted, meticulously detailed and replete with richly developed characters."
— LONDON FREE PRESS

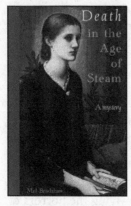

Death in the Age of Steam
978-1894917001
$22.95

Toronto in 1856 is industrializing with little time for scruple or sentiment. When Reform politician William Sheridan dies suddenly and his daughter Theresa vanishes, only one man persists in asking questions. A former suitor of Theresa's, bank cashier Isaac Harris has never managed to forget her, despite her marriage to another man. Thrust into the role of amateur detective, he must now struggle with the demands of his job and the shortcomings of the fledgling city police. He also faces the hostility of Theresa's powerful husband, a steamboat and railway magnate. Harris's search takes a grisly turn when he finds human remains decked in traces of Theresa's finery. If she is dead, who is responsible? And who cares to find out, apart from the man who wooed her too timidly and now would do anything to make up for it? This novel whirls the reader through a richly realized Victorian landscape, from Niagara Falls to Montreal to the shores of Lake Superior.

"This is a delightful, romance, mystery, and detective story, full of history and brimming with intelligent and superbly-rendered characters."
— W.P. KINSELLA

VISIT US AT

Dundurn.com
Definingcanada.ca
@dundurnpress
Facebook.com/dundurnpress